Wish, by Duncan Sayarer

Redchop

Leah was a girl of less than a quarter of age. Little as she was, at this time of the year she lived by the tall window halfway up the stairs, when the days are short and the nights long it was here away from family life that she found peace and quiet. For days and weeks and months, she would stare out into the whiteness laid down by the winter sky over Vikvalda and all of the earth. The sharp and jagged blanket of frost and ice brought the whole world to a halt, and all appeared still. The stillness to an untrained eye could be confused for lifelessness, the harsh temperatures narrowing the vision and hearts of many as the winter binds all in gloom. But not little Leah, with her youthfully adept and sparkling eyes of a mesmerising blue, she knew what to look for in this seemingly suffocating white, for this was how she spent all of her winters. Tucked into her fluffy reindeer coat stitched together by her now gone grandmother, she would sit and lay all winter on this ledge by the window, awake or otherwise. Draped in the warming furs and her tresses of wavy blonde hair, she would sit by the window watching the wintry world with unusual eagerness, and in any rare moment of boredom, weave her glorious locks into long plaits like that of the mooring ropes used at a ship's docking.

Gazing through the warped and imperfect glass she observed with eyes shining, not yet narrowed by age, changes taking place so slight and slow that they would be ignored and unnoticed by adults of stiffer heart. Every year she witnessed the first snows melt on the corner of the Grain Mill's roof directly opposite Redchop church. Its eastward facing clock towered above the horizon and it rang so loudly none could ever forget the time. Its glass would magnify the mellow wintry sun onto the front of the Grain Mill, just warm enough that right there, weeks before the rest of the land, the first movements would begin with a drip and a drop and a gentle tapping sound as the winter began to melt, gradually forming puddles between the snow-covered cobbles below. The local birds of Redchop would hover above the Grain Mill, always a certain source of food for them in the harsher seasons when there was no hanging berry on bush or early worm to hunt. When the puddles grew large enough and shone the same colour as the sky, the birds would swoop down to wash themselves for the first time in many months, splashing and flapping with songs, heralding to all in the village that spring was now coming, but the village would never take any notice of them. The adults continued on just as they had done every day before, blind and disinterested in anything that was neither food nor money. The adults of Redchop preferred to wait for the newspaper or radio, or their friends to announce spring's arrival, it was easier that way. They would never risk an early or incorrect statement that might cost them a compliment at the dinner table. While the adults worked day in and day out each month, waiting for their news,

Leah would be witness to all the curious changes that nature pursues four times per year - the muddling and smearing of colour, temperature and smell between the glorious gifts that are the seasons. As the colours changed and sounds of movement echoed across the stillness, the landscape would begin to shift and roll as the blanket of snow and ice merged with the soil and turned itself into the nourishing streams of spring.

It was around this time that the first smile of the year would creep from Leah's stomach to chest and then onto her fine lips - that feeling she had felt buried deep inside and anticipated for months. The warmth of spring brought Leah joy and excitement as she watched the birds share her understanding of change. She wouldn't however let any of the adults see her glee, they didn't deserve her smiles she thought, for they would never share their own with her. Leah knew that not more than a dozen mornings from now the whole of Redchop would wake one day to find church bells ringing and green in place of white. The adults would see and hear it all at once, listening to the well-practised and clear voices on the radio, and reading the newspapers which explained how colourful everything was in a black and white font. They read, "The spring has arrived!" This was how it worked for the adults of Redchop, and Leah could never understand why they preferred things this way – to her it was completely unsatisfying and encapsulated everything about adults that annoyed her.

Leah preferred having something to think about whilst she plaited her hair. She preferred things around her to be a little unclear, very unclear in fact. She liked it that way, thrived on it, and this was most true when it came to her and relationships with others. She didn't have many friends; she couldn't keep them. She often created corners and obstacles solely for the sake of issue, unintentionally of course. Situations of apparent chaos would manifest to draw her attention from an unresolved internal drama which roamed freely behind her blue eyes. Leah required constant distractions, constant external stimuli and drama, be it people, plant or animal - and it was this state of being that was the essence of her tireless and boundless curiosity. This compulsion to not know, to never be sure or clear of anything was the consequence of something distasteful in her past. It was, however, beheld as a gift in the present. It guaranteed her the intoxicating and overwhelmingly pleasurable experience of wondering, and it gave her the useful ability to forget and ignore anything immediate or negative.

Being the dreamer that she was, exploration was the best source of stimulation for Leah, even if it brought with it fear and danger. She often found herself in trouble at school, in friendships and in play. To her elders, Leah appeared nonchalant, a little lost and at the same time, rather shy. The presumptuously blind eyes of adulthood simply saw a youthful blonde beauty, blue eyed and innocent. They saw as they chose and did not consider what may motivate her behaviour. Presumptuousness is of course, a valuable skill of the initiated alone.

Leah, though, was indeed a peculiar girl and she seemed that way to most, even to her mother who, in direct contrast to Leah, had lost touch with anything other than her immediate and obvious self. She sought constant, absolute and meticulous categorisation of all aspects of life and the lives of those around her. She lived in fear of anything unexpected, which in turn stamped out all involvement of dreaming and what could be considered spontaneous pleasures from her life. Leah couldn't stand her mother's presence - she radiated stress, her methodical planning was a threat to Leah's own curious state of existence. Leah rejected any attempts at control. It was her own lack of governance that helped her to ignore whatever it was that nagged and tugged inside of her chest when she was alone. Any extended time together between Leah and her mother inevitably resulted in blistering conflict and tantrum, so they avoided each other and sat in different areas of the house.

To the right of the window ledge where Leah was sitting, hanging on a plainly painted wall, there was a photo of her mother in her younger years. So similar her and Leah were, at this same age. The same flowing hair and piercing blue eyes, same slightly upturned and adventurous nose, same shape of mouth gilded with the same well-defined rose-pink lips - it was almost like a mirror pointing straight at her. Sitting through the long and slow winters Leah would stare and study her mother in this photograph, both outside and in. She preferred to spend time with her mother in this way - from a safe distance. *"Why has she become the way she is?"* Leah thought to herself, *"She's always doing something peculiar"* and she imagined her long scaly fingers bent with frustration. *"She's always busy with something unnecessary, always moving and always spoiling any who dare come close to her"* she thought. Her mother never seemed to have any time for her, or for laughter or for joy, and whenever the two shared company all Leah could ever do was smile for her mother's sake. It was quite a burden for a child.

The photo was placed on the wall over the stairs in such a way that anyone coming down from the bedrooms would see it clearly looking at them, and that, Leah thought, was why it was hung there - her mother was once beautiful and blonde and full of hope for life and that must be remembered and constantly reminded to all. Leah pondered on as she did, and the winter day progressed onwards just as it had started. The bustle of the street paled into monotony for all involved and as the night inevitably fell, things became quieter still, only the moon was awake to hear the fox snigger and cackle at those who sleep and miss the dancing of the stars. Leah stayed up quite late, but she dozed off just after midnight.

The next morning, she awoke around the same time as usual, the warm and heartening smell of bread from the local bakery her only company before the clock's hands turned to the hour, and the bronze bells rang for work. She opened her eyes. Blue sky shone through the window and droplets of moisture rolled down the glass like pearls, a prism of yellows, blues and white as they captured and fractured the colours from the outdoor wintery glow. Her arms were comfortably wrapped around herself and one of her large plaits that she must have fallen asleep whilst weaving, cuddling it like a pillow. It was a needed loyal friend whilst she slept. She gave a slight purring yawn, stretching out her arms and legs and spreading her toes. She rubbed her face, opened her eyes and ears and listened for the songs from the birds that she knew would be flapping and playing in the puddle at this time. Her anticipation was eager and great, but there was no such sound to be heard. There was no bird song, just the all too familiar sound of snow and ice crunching under boot, the mumbling of morning groans, coughs and yawns as the older folk of Redchop came one by one into the street and went about their early morning rituals, fetching bread and milk and the local paper before moving on to their places of work. "*Where are the birds and the flapping and where are the songs?*" she said to herself with an anxious whisper. Immediately falling into a frenzy as her anticipations for this moment had suddenly fallen short, she sat bolt upright and placed her small fingers onto the window ledge, her face was close enough to the ice cold glass that her nose felt a pinching chill and mist followed her breathing. The droplets that had gathered themselves at the base of the window, waiting for an excuse to clump together, rolled onto her fingers a cold sensation as she looked to the corner of the Grain Mill to see no puddle, no birds, and only deep disappointment.

A group of adults stood there by the corner of the mill, huddled together smoking and talking and doing everything older people do. *"What are they doing? What are they doing there!"* Leah muttered with smite as a childish anger crumpled her face to ruin the sweet smile that she had gone to sleep with. She became anxious, something was wrong. *"The Spring has stopped!"* She said with panic through clenched lips. This reality twitched at her neck and shoulders and she screamed inside. Leah's chest was pounding and her shallow breathing was chaining her into a claustrophobic state. Her head was spinning, and she felt faint as her emotions became overwhelming, running through her, wrecking everything that she had been patiently waiting for all winter. For so many years Leah had witnessed the birds bring the spring and they were always, always on time. She knew they would play for a few days before the changes became more noticeable. She knew that after the birds came to the Grain Mill that within a few mornings the squirrels would begin their mischief and play above the village, knocking the snow from the trees, rooftops and telegraph wires onto the frustrated adults' heads and that this was the same every single year without fail. She had waited patiently for this for months, just like always. She longed to see the spring so she could smile. Long before the newspapers told everyone else to do so, before the adults ruined it all for her like they always ruined everything.

Leah jumped down from her ledge by the window and onto the stairs, she ran down quickly not worrying of splinters, her little feet patting the wooden boards to announce her movements to any who listened or cared, no one did. Her haste was so that she couldn't find the time for her favourite canvas shoes, which smiled with red leather stitching, again a gift from her beloved grandmother. She skipped over them at the bottom of the stairs. Panicking, she ran across the red clay tiles which the kitchen sat tidily upon, skidding on a mat and successfully navigating around the hot cast iron stove that would warm the house all year round. She ran on into the storeroom. She ran down past long rows of tinned produce and winter supplies, past her father's tool bench and her mother's gardening chest from which protruded many a sharp hazard. She ran hands first straight into the large and untreated oak door at the end of the storeroom, hung on rusted iron hinges it reluctantly creaked and screeched in displeasure as she heaved with all her might to get outside into the street. Running quickly now, the bitter cold of snow and ice thrashed and burned her bare feet, but she couldn't feel it, such was her mood of urgency. She ran over to the Mill. Pushing people out of the way she could see the puddle was frozen solid, and above where dripping waters had been there were now sharp knives of ice pointing menacingly at her. Disappointment and sadness drenched her eyes, all she had longed to see today had vanished before it had even appeared. *"No!"* she screamed aloud, now for the first time letting her feelings out. She turned with a childish stamp and she ran on again. The adults mingled back together as though nothing of significance had happened. *"Kids!"* one of them chuckled through a cloud of cigarette smoke.

Running onwards, the only place she knew to go to now was her friends - well, her only real friend - Nihal. His house sat on the edge of town. She would go straight there now. *"Nihal will understand me, he always understands me"* she thought, he would help her to make sense of her emotions and help her to calm down. Leah ran down Redchop high street. It cut through the centre of the village at an angle and was lined with gas lamps and hanging boards advertising local commerce, no greenery or flowers this time of year. She scurried on, past and through many groups of people that barely noticed the small barefooted girl running in the snow, dragging her oversized coat and plaited blonde hair behind her, like a sledge she left a trail. Her commotion was not at all felt by others.

Running to the end of the high street and a left, she could now see ahead where she was going. Nihal's house stood on the edge of town as one of the last before the flattened land of farming began, his parents and parents' parents had always worked the fields. The house itself was old and crooked, made of wood and thatch and rusted nails, it carried a charm that only something of age and slight dysfunction could carry. She ran down the snow-covered drive, her toes kissing the pebbles that lived below as they rumbled in step. Past the front door she went and then around to the side of the house, through the courtyard and on to the barn where she knew she would find her friend. She soon reached the barn and using all of her weight, she leant back pulling the rope handle to open one of the large wooden doors. Leah ran inside. There in the centre of the barn she found what she was looking for, her friend Nihal. He lay sprawled out asleep on a stack of hay next to his three small dogs, also happily sleeping. *"Nihal! Nihal! Wake up!"* Leah ran into the dark, dusty and cob-webbed barn and insisted that her friend wake up by shaking him from side to side. Giving only a groan and a mumble, Nihal was a solid sleeper and had been working hard in the barn the day before and indeed all winter. *"Nihal! wake up!"* Leah pleaded with her sleeping friend but to no avail. She looked around and saw that he was also bare foot. Pulling his big toe Leah managed to get some response and Nihal sprang up *"Ouch! What what! What's wrong, what's happening ?"* He alerted, and she plunged herself into his face, *"The spring has stopped Nihal! The birds have gone, they have gone! They came and went but left us with no signs of spring and I don't know what to do!"* Leah's emotions were so glaringly strong and animated that they assured all in the barn, Nihal, his dogs and the raven perched on a rafter above, that it was indeed correct to be concerned. Nihal trusted his friend and he too had something to add *"I was just dreaming Leah, I was just dreaming about a very long winter. I was dreaming that the spring would come late, that my father's crops didn't sprout and that we went on an adventure to find out why. I was just dreaming about it."* finished Nihal.

A wind boldly ripped its way into the barn and flung the doors wide, snapping the wooden baton used to hold them secure, tossing hay and dust into the air and swirling in the centre of the barn as sun light shone through the haze like a solid wall of light, projecting a granular image of a mountain before them. *"That's Mt Arackach!"* shouted Leah feeling some relief as a little magic and mystique returned to obscure their seemingly bleak situation. The misty image grew in size and detail before their eyes as the force of the wind strengthened, hurling itself frantically throughout the barn, searching all of its corners for dust and debris to toss and fold before them. They both watched and were mesmerised and chilled to their core. Nihal's dogs began to bark and became excitable, they ran and jumped into the dusty light. Their frolicking and snapping dispersed the wind, fracturing and scattering the image into all corners of the room. The wind continued to blow strongly and drove the dust to the walls of the barn, swirling and hissing like an angered snake, it twisted itself through cracks in the walls and missing tiles on the barn roof to leave the room as it had found it. The image was now completely gone and the wind had ground to a halt - slamming the doors as it left. The room fell dark and still, silence collapsed itself upon them.

"*Leah*" Nihal, a tallish and scruffy dark blonde-haired boy with greyish eyes spoke to his friend "*Leah, I think the wind was in my dream too, the same wind came into my dream and showed me Mt Arackach, we went there together and found some clues to help us find....*" Nihal stopped mid-sentence, rubbing his eyes and squinting. He had gotten some hay blown in them and was struggling to rub them clean. Leah paused in her thoughts and stepped back to consider Nihal's dream and the message of the winds. She now had something to ponder again and a few doors in her mind swung pleasantly open. She looked down at the dogs playing with one another on the barn floor. Above her head the raven leapt from its perch and flew out of the barn doors with wings spread wide.

There was a strong sensation in Leah, present in all her body, a feeling of spontaneity and rush, an urgency telling her to act immediately before the moment was lost. She felt pushed and drawn by something she had not in memory felt before. She was curious, confused, and certain all at once - it hurt a little. Something powerful was beckoning her. Drawing her away from Redchop, her and her friend, now, right now! "*Go and run into the forests and to the Mountain of Arackach. Go into the outside world to find the Spring and find the answers that you may seek,*" the feelings spoke to her loudly. She was enchanted! She didn't need to consider what may happen or why. "*Come on Nihal,*" she took her friend's hand, interrupting his eye rubbing, and they ran! "*Let's go Nihal! Let's go to find the spring and your dream, let's go to Mt. Arackach to find out what happens there*". She took his hand and they ran. Nihal gathered his steps together clumsily, still squinting. With his free hand he grabbed two scarves that hung from one of the old rusty hooks next to the door and they ran together bare foot out of the barn and into the snowy courtyard. *"Leah I don't have any shoes on. Leah, where are your shoes?"* Nihal asked between breaths, confused. *"We don't have time Nihal! We are going now!"* Leah insisted in an urgent tone that matched her stride. They ran out off into a late Vikvalda winter, still of biting cold and frost. In half a moment the cold air had whipped their cheeks red and their unprotected feet were tender not long after. Hearts pulsing strongly, there was no time to think or feel anything, only their emotions were true. Holding hands they ran up the drive and Nihal waved over his shoulder to his dogs that sat three abreast in the barn doorway, watching with wide eyes and slanted heads, as if confused by their hasty decision, they watched the two friends move further away into the winter.

They ran on into the street, past the fields that in summer would be ripe, lush and wonderful for playing sunny games, now just flat and sprawling, smothered by a blanket of ice and snow. After running and stumbling for a short while, they reached the end of the farmlands. They began to slow to a walking pace. Catching what few breaths from the air that he could Nihal gasped, *"What's happening now Leah? Are we going to Mt Arackach?"* Nihal asked freshly in haste.

He had been inspired by his dream and by Leah's infectious enthusiasm. They were going to do this together! He thought. *"Yes, we must go to the mountain, we must find what is there, we must find the spring. We must find the answer!"* confirmed Leah resolutely. *"Answer to what Leah? I've never heard you so certain of anything before. Besides, there are no roads to the mountain. The roads stop after the last cart track in the far field. There are no paths going that way, that's why no one goes there"* stated Nihal. *"Maybe it's the other way around Nihal"* said Leah, *"all paths must be trodden a first time. Let's go!"*.

They continued onwards for several days. Trudging through snow and peat and a very cold mud that tickled as it rolled around their small toes. As they moved further from Redchop they could see Mt Arackach towering above them. Without any roads it served as their guide and compass, indeed it felt as though it was watching over them and providing some much needed authority, in a world governed by emotions and youth.

Mt. Arackach

The two friends had moved far enough from Redchop to see the winter had grown noticeably older and a little less competent in its bite. It was visible on the tips of the trees and the hedgerows, and beneath their feet now was the regular occurrence of mud, a soggy fibrous mix of earth and plant matter that back in town had been covered in snow and frozen solid like a speckled black granite. The further away from Redchop they were, and the closer to the Mountain they ventured, the warmer it seemed to become. It was only slightly noticeable to them, they still felt cold, but to the land the slightest change can affect many forms. As they walked, the two friends talked things over, discussing all that had happened. Leah bent the truth a lot, tending to sensationalise everything although not purposefully. It was merely her rich emotions and perceptions of any given situation, a manifestation of her dreaminess and her escapism. Nihal on the other hand was usually rather blunt, and lovably so. He found himself pleasantly secure in the apparent and the obvious, he liked to keep things simple. The two personalities complemented one another like night and day, and as a whole brought a consensus to their moods, albeit the occasional conflict, too.

A few days later, with the sun high in the centre of a blue sheet of sky, things suddenly felt much warmer. The burning of the sun was now strong enough to quickly thin and disperse the clouds of moisture that gathered with their breath and make supple their tender skin and cracked lips. Nihal stopped and said *"can you feel that Leah? There are signs of spring here it seems"*. Leah nodded without saying anything and came to a halt two paces later. *"Yes, I had noticed too. There was a trickling stream a few miles back that would have been frozen in the temperatures back home"* she said in a thoughtful way. Days of walking and exposure to the elements had calmed her commotion a little, she was feeling quite relaxed and altogether more content than she had been a few mornings prior. *"Were the birds wrong?"* asked Nihal in a trusting way. *"That's impossible, the birds are never wrong; they always arrive before the clock and the bells!"* insisted Leah. Nihal spoke innocently once more *"Were you wrong Leah, were you wrong about the spring not coming? And was my dream just a dream too? Just a dream to ignore like my dad tells me.?"* Leah turned to her friend looking a little hopeless, stumped by Nihal's simple questioning on a matter she had shared since seeing the stream flowing a few miles prior. *"I don't know Nihal! How am I supposed to know?"* she pleaded. *"Of course your dad would say that anyway! He is too busy to notice the birds doing the same thing every single year! Adults never pay any attention to anything that matters. The birds always know first so when they were not there I got scared because, because I don't know why! I got upset and I wanted to see you, then we saw it all altogether. Remember? The wind showed us the mountain, the wind was in your dream too!"* She continued *"You're right Nihal, the spring is coming we can see it here, but that must be because of the mountain, there must be something up there and we can't turn back now!"*

Leah's calmness ended abruptly with Nihal's probing, and she got carried away with her explanation. She became upset and the last few words were spoken with a tearful tone. She remembered the feelings she had felt in the barn and how strong they were. How potent. It can't have been meaningless, she thought to herself. Nihal sensed this and hobbled over giving her a hug as her good friend. *"You are my best friend and I want to come with you,"* Nihal said. He was always very generous, often unconsciously suppressing his own true feelings for others' sake. *"I am not sure about the spring now but my dream was real and I think the mountain will be exciting too. How are we going to get up there though?"* he asked, and they cast their heads upwards towards the mountain.

Mt. Arackach stood at the centre of Vikvalda. It towered above the forests and farmlands, the only piece of earth capable of threatening the sky. Back in Redchop a certain mythology surrounded it, it existed in the schools and libraries and it was inscribed on Redchop's flag and local currency. Steep cliffs on one side and rolling hills with valleys and streams on the other, it was a representation of all that is hope and all that is fear. At its summit were both swirling black clouds and the bluest of sky. Ice cold winds hurtled down the mountain's western face, but its eastern side channelled a moist and warmer air, picking up foliage from the shrubbery that lived at its base and pushing it into the flatlands where the two friends stood. *"Can you feel that Nihal? Like I said, it must be the mountain that brought the spring here."* said Leah, opening her arms wide to embrace the wind that rolled down the mountainside. It rubbed itself over her chilled skin, the warm air massaging her body and encouraging blood to flow, bringing with it a relaxing sensation that she hadn't felt since last autumn. This mountain wind descended upon any who came close, it was strong and persistent, it governed. Mt Arackach's size was such that it generated its own climate, a separate world within the otherwise half frozen woodlands and the bleak flattened fields that stretch out towards Redchop.

Mt Arackach was a special place. There were many tales back home, often shared at the dinner table or overheard in bars where alcohol flowed and inhibitions dwindled. Tales of the mountain's secrets were commonplace. Magic and spirits were added by any narrator for effect and depending how drunk they were, ghosts too. But the mountain's true message was of creation and destruction. It was said that any who could stomach its teachings and carry it on their shoulders through life would acquire power and strength not known to the common man, but that such knowledge could not be held without risk. The true teachings of Mt Arackach, it was said, could undermine one's desire to live in this world.

At its base, the eastern flank was rich and dense, watered by regular precipitation and warmed by the flowing winds. The plant life here served as do the stones in the damming of a lake, channelling energy that coalesces and assumes an amplified and consistent path. Gales carved valleys through the trees and shrubs that lay along the base, howling as it tore a path through their branches. Over the centuries the wind had sculpted a tunnel through the woodland and at the far end could be seen the foot of the mountain, where the ground rose sharply upwards. They looked straight on along this scar running through the woods, inviting them in. The path to Mt Arackach was now before them. They looked at one another, hugged, and moved on ahead through the steep wooded archways.

Wooden Arches

Here in the woodland, the mountain wind had blown warm for long enough that life had begun to turn a pleasant and colourful corner. The colours surrounding Leah and Nihal were many months ahead of what was seasonal, the scenery was sprinkled with bright flowers, petals, buds and leaves all competing desperately for their attention. It was like nothing they had seen before, especially at this time of year. The plants were local only to this area it seemed, the rich mineral waters and warm mountain winds having designed things entirely from scratch – it was quite unique and wonderful. The air was tinted with the dusty taste and smell of a variety of sweet pollens which faintly tickled in their noses, a joyful sensation. "*Achoo!*" They both sneezed as a consequence. The plants frolicked with blossoms, and they all brandished themselves recklessly together. Leah and Nihal walked straight along this winding channel of colours - greens and blues, pinks and violets either side. On they went into the wind that warmed them through to their bone-marrow, easing their aching winter chilled muscles and encouraging them to feel good about what they were doing. Any pessimism that may have existed between the two had now gone. Looking a few metres into the woodland either side of where they stood, they could see the icy air still prowled like a hungry wolf, a harsh and cold winter still lived close by. An unnerving feeling of something unnatural vexed their senses between pleasure and discomfort as they continued towards the foot of the mountain, following what the wind had clearly designed for any who chose this path.

The two friends arrived at a fork in the way. At this point gales had blown around a large tree creating enough turbulence to alter the trunk's direction of growth. Bent over itself and hollowed out by a lifetime of uncertainty it hunched over itself like an old and wretched man, buckled from the roots up, its trunk confused countless times by ever-changing winds, each twist apparent in its lacerated bark and visible from every angle. Only the tip of the longest branch had settled upon a direction, and it pointed clearly to the left of where they stood. The path running to the left side of the tree was furnished with a fine assortment of gems, pebbles and stones, all of different size and colour and shape, some of matt and others of polished shine. They had been cast down the mountain by wind and rain over many years and now laid here to rest, muddling amongst themselves.

After walking barefoot for so long, a gem stone and fine pebble path would surely be like a fine silk beneath their sore feet. *"Should we travel this way to the base of the mountain? It really looks easier."* Nihal said encouragingly, suggesting the direction by pointing his finger as he spoke. To the right, in the opposite direction to which the wind had curled the tree, lay a less clear path, an area naturally abandoned in favour of another and left to grow feral. For the two friends, it didn't look anywhere near as inviting. Having directed them this far, they decided that the wind was there to be trusted and they should continue to follow it. *"Let's take this stony path over here Leah"* said Nihal again, *"the wind has made the way for us like it made the way here. Like it came to the barn back home."* he finished, still pointing. Leah said nothing, smiled with a corner of her lip and followed Nihal's finger with her feet. They both walked on together.

As they moved onwards down the stony path the wind died down a little. With the eastern air absent it was a little cooler, but still it seemed much warmer than it had been in the farmlands back home. Patches of spring were now cropping up by regular means, and small plants were acting with confidence on the slight hint of lasting warmth. Not all the trees were convinced however, the spring had not arrived for all fairly. Only the youngest shrub and plant, the less wise ran out with no clothes, exposing themselves to the slightest change, naive and vulnerable, but they would feel it first. The older more experienced trees lay patiently in wait until all frost, all doubt, was banished, and the winter completely gone, not to return for many months. On the day that the oldest trees finally gave in to change, the earth would sing a merry song. The birds, the air, the leaves and the insects would all hum together and sing a fantastic hymn, an orchestra of life vibrating energy into the sky.

Nihal and Leah wandered on. By this point they had both become a little tired. Their dreams and emotions had driven them impulsively out into the cold unprepared, and they were lucky to have gotten this far unchallenged by health or hunger. Many miles they'd trodden bare foot, no skin of beast to break their fall, their small feet were worn and tender. "*I think I need to rest now,*" said Nihal. It was the first time a rest had been mentioned or even considered by either of them. " *Yes me too*" agreed an equally exhausted Leah "*Let's just stop here then.*" Without hesitation and with a thud, they both immediately sat themselves down in a cropping of long grass among which was strewn the most appropriate array of pink and blue flowers. Three huge trees towered above them, magnificent, wise and hospitable. Sheltering them as best they could without their leafy summer coats, they reassured the two friends with swaying, creaking, arthritic groans. The trees communicated deeply and softly the message that they were here for mankind's protection, to help humans complete their task on earth. "*I think the spring is almost here now,*" spoke Leah. Looking around, although not completely uniform, the signs were becoming undeniable. The sky gasped a breath. "*Listen Nihal, listen,*" Leah instructed. They could hear the chorus of spring all around them. The hairs on their arms and neck stood on end as the spring entered through all of their senses and nourished their hearts. The song of pre-summer filled the air, as all on the earth began their well-choreographed celebration of rebirth. The same song was sung at home for the spring fair, "*It's the nectar of life, the voice of awakening,"* it began, *"The spring! The new! The Sun! Stand up and sing, the Spring!"* Everything rang through them. Their skin and ears and eyes. Their minds were enlightened by an experience that can only be enjoyed after a little suffering. The winter and its gloom were gone for the year. *"Hoorah for The Spring!"* They both shouted. Behind them the mountain sat still towering up into the sky, shooting up above the tallest tree and clouds, sitting there jagged and bold whilst smiling at them, it commanded the respect and attention of all.

The flurry of energy found a home in the core of Leah's tenacious personality, and she suddenly forgot all of her tiredness. *"We must go on again soon, we have a long way to go still,"* she whispered feeling inspired, but in a quiet voice so as not to disturb the wildlife that now surrounded them. *"But I'm too tired Leah. We should rest here for the rest of the day. We have walked really far now. Let's just rest now Leah. The trees will take care of us here, it's quite sheltered. I just want to rest."* Leah's mood was mutable, and she didn't pressure her friend. A sharp wind picked up suddenly and tugged at their clothes, blowing any loose thread from their seams. Upwards it belched, off and into the surrounding foliage.

It parted next to them an opening, brushing aside a large conifer tree's outer layers which splashed down a brief but heavy cold shower. The trees still carried water this time of year, their coat of snow having only just melted away. The wind revealed an evergreen blanket of moss like freshly picked cotton underneath the branches, like a miniature landscape similar to any hillside from a distance. Nihal and Leah had both missed this event, they were both asleep. Warmer and safer than they had been at any time since leaving, a comfortable exhaustion had taken them away.

The next morning, Nihal awoke suddenly *"Leah"* he called, nudging her shoulder. *"Get up, look!"* Leah woke and opened an eye to find both her feet dangling beneath her and most certainly not where she had last put them. Not quite awake enough to be shocked but shocked enough to be awake, she shook her head a few times quickly to throw off some of the morning's daze and grasp what was occurring. She then opened her other eye, realising it may help in making head or tail of this unusual situation. The rubbing of both eyes with her palms cleared the fog and to her amazement, she realised she and Nihal were now atop Mt Arackach, at the highest point in all the land of Vikvalda! Leah tried to force calm on herself yet failed dramatically. *"The Mountain! Sir Arackach, we are here!"* she shouted.

On the summit of the mountain was the first piece of land to be created by the earth, many millions of years before. Old earth untouched by farmers, it was of a different texture and colour to that of the forest and farmland. Soft and crumbly like half milled grain and with a fine grass top, it was extremely comfy to be sat upon.

"*Wow!*" said Nihal, who had also been in a semi-conscious state. He struggled to find many words and Leah gave him no time. "*Shhhh,*" she hissed, placing a finger on his lips. "*Quiet Nihal, we are atop Sir Arackach, we can see everything, all of Vikvalda can be seen from here! Look, there is Redchop. They'll be sat looking at the mountain and wishing they were up here!*" She pointed across the horizon expressing her excitement, forgetting she had just told Nihal to be quiet. "*How did we get up here? It must have been the wind again. There's no other way. It must have brought us here whilst we slept! I knew it! I knew there was a reason. The sky and clouds they are going to show us why we are here!*" she said, completely forgetting that the Spring had already arrived in the woods below. Leah surrendered to her emotions as usual, a pleasant and fickle joy began to flow through her. So carried away in the moment was she that she didn't realise she had shifted from her perpetual pondering and mystery to something closer to that of the satisfaction in resoluteness. She promptly stood up and beamed a bright and toothy smile. "*Okay!*" she shouted in welcome to the morning. Her shouting was sharp and feminine and shot across the mountainside like lightning, falling off the cliffs and echoing as it fell, it disturbed the local wildlife in the valley beneath. Far below, birds flew and horses bolted through the grass; their movements resembled that of ripples surrounding a stone thrown in an otherwise peaceful lake. Leah looked out into the morning which now presented itself to her and Nihal in startling and fantastic clarity.

To the left, half of the sky above Mt Arackach was clear and blue with a finely scattered mist along its waistline where the heavens were shackled to the earth. The sun's rays shone strongly onto their faces - at this altitude their pale wintry skin was sensitive and reddened quickly. To their right the sky had a different mood. Clouds bellowed over this greying part of the Vikvalda horizon, where the farmlands sat cold and still in a dark and dull whiteness due to the continuing shortage of warmth from the sun. Nothing moved there, all was quite bleak and miserable. They stood for a while, their heads shifting from side to side as they looked at the surreal contrast between left and right - words that before they had used only in the context of direction. This partitioned sky, cleft in such a way that it did look entirely unnatural, was something that could only be witnessed from here on Mt Arackach, and this was why it held such special precedence in the tales told back home at Redchop.

The mountain's banks were so vast, steep and angular that the cold air hurtling down its western walls would steal air from above and part the sky, splitting it seamlessly into left and right, east and west - the clouds caged and confined light and dark to either side. The summit of Mt Arackach, the central point between fear and hope. Winds blew strongly all around, it swept up small clouds that had strayed from the bulging herd and tossed them together; they shrank and contracted flattening out into both common and unnatural forms. Cross winds waited their turn before hurrying in on the action, roughing out the air

- the clouds responded by erecting great grey pillars framed with crumpled white ridges. The two friends watched the turbulence illustrate every mood and emotion possible. The sky above Mt Arackach was a living landscape of its own. The entire universe could be seen! *"What is that?"* Nihal said, pointing at one of the briefly recognisable shapes in the sky *"I have no idea,"* replied Leah, in a drawn out and amazed tone. They stood with mouths open, nothing but bewildered spectators of a chaotic theatre.

The clouds continued their dance, briefly assuming recognisable forms only to be again shattered by the wonderful chaos that created and destroyed for fun. Nihal looked down at Redchop, a stark contrast to the energy and amazement seen in the sky above them. This enriching experience swelled in his heart and although he felt spiritually aroused, he could only manage a characteristically common question. *"Why do we even live in towns Leah? It's so boring compared to this. I would just be down there in my barn with my doggies now, oh I do miss my dogs. Up here I feel so alive, even more alive than my last birthday party!"* Nihal went on, sweetly. Leah responded sullenly, almost bitterly. After seeing all they had this morning, she was saddened by the thought of her mundane life back home, the life that she knew one day she would have to return to. *"It's the adults Nihal, they need their stability and their predictability. They can't live otherwise. They are too scared of all of this and their own thoughts and feelings and memories. They have to surround themselves with the familiar and the self-flattering. But this is not why we are here, Nihal"* she said. *"Why are we here?"* asked Nihal innocently. After all, the spring had already arrived. Leah frowned gently knowing Nihal was being as he was. *"You know why we are here. We are here because the wind brought us here and we are looking for a clue as to why that is. Let's go and find it!"* she concluded. With a confident step backwards from the edge of the mountain, she announced it was time for them to leave.

Womblot

"You look for clues and talk of leaving but I say you've only just arrived! Does it smell that bad here, are you to hide, or will you enjoy the ride?" a high pitched and chirpy voice rhymed its way up past their shoulders, causing both Nihal and Leah to jump. *"Oh hello"* said Nihal. Looking down towards the ground, there in the gap between him and Leah stood a mountain gnome wearing baggy brown corduroy trousers and a blazer embroidered with green silk lettering of some unknown and artful script. On his feet, black leather pumps with red laces, and over his shoulder, a canvas satchel. A wonky hat sat upon his head slanted to the left with a bunch of dried acorns attached to its peak. His long, dark red hair curled around its brim as well as his freckled, rosy cheeks and ears.

He stood there as if he had been part of a trio and one of their friends, just sat there listening the whole time. *"Hello, my name is Womblot and welcome to Womblotian!"* he smiled and offered both his hands to each of the friends, crossing his arms to offer left to right side and right to left. *"I'm Nihal,"* said Nihal taking his hand, *"And my name's Leah. nice to meet you Mr Womblot,"* said Leah following suit.

Arms linked and crossed between the three like a magic triangle, they held hands together. *"In Womblotian we shake on a count of four, not three"* said Womblot, and they shook together a trusting shake - out loud, *"One, two, three and four!"*

Womblot sat himself down and began to speak. *"So tell me, how are you both?"* He swung his legs out in front of him and jiggled like a child playing on a swing. *"I hear you've begun a long journey, it's not yet clear, but it's what I hear and, if you believe you'll win then are you really gambling?"* The wind whistled its way round the three of them and scuffled Leah's long hair into her face. *"Hear from who?"* said Nihal suspiciously. *"Why, from you!"* pronounced Womblot with an amused nod and a matter-of-fact tone. *"I sit here most days, doing my fishing, it keeps me informed of the ways of the winds and that's my job,"* Womblot said, picking up a long drail wood cane that was laying behind him and thrust it out over the side of the mountain into the wind that continued to blow. Long tassels made of horse hairs and silk dangled neatly from its tip and wriggled like enchanted snakes in the gales that were flung against the cliff side. *"Fishing? We're on a mountain, and there's no hook, what are you going to catch?"* asked Nihal. *"Fishing? Hook? Catch? Who in their right mind would use a hook to catch? Catch catch the Ar-a-ckatch - hummm."* Womblot giggled. *"Here we do not plan, the outcome would be too predictable. Here we do not catch, not on Arackach. We only watch and let things be, we wait, we let things come and that's what we see,"* Womblot finished and stuffed the cane into the thin soil and wiggled it around in search of a supporting gap in the rocks beneath. Happy it was stable and leaning at the correct angle, he let go. His hands now free, he closed his eyes, straightened his arms and lifted his shoulders, doing some sort of pre-exercise stretches or warmup. He inhaled and then exhaled deeply, three times over. All four of his limbs were now sprawled ahead jovially into the mountain air. *"What do you mean, 'we'?"* asked Leah. *"Are there more of you here? And do you know something about the spring and the wind. We are looking for the reason why we are here."* nudging Nihal with her shoulder looking for some support and assurance that she was not the only one confused by all this. *"Yes. Yes, I had a dream and it showed me the mountain. We were looking for the spring, though I am not sure we are any longer?"* he said, subtly returning command of the conversation back to Leah. Her lips curled a little and she frowned with reluctant agreement, the journey for spring no longer made any sense given that the air had already warmed and the flowers had bloomed.

Womblot giggled away *"Oh no not I, when we say I we mean we, but I is we when I talk of philosophy, for the I in philosophy is the we in wedding. There are, as always, lots of others to consider –"* Leah and Nihal looked at each other as Womblot continued on with his riddle and rhyme *"--the we in wedding is the he in she and the ear in earth. You ask for clues and you ask me too, I know of only a few, but they are not mine to deliver and nor can I know, it is why I take my cane, and.... throw,"* Womblot picked up his cane again and cast it out. Matching all the mannerisms of a fisherman at sea, he sat still watching the wind blowing and happily rhyming out his verses.

Leah and Nihal stared out over the cliff edge watching the tassels on Womblot's cane twist and flutter like blowing leaves cornered between two houses, Womblot's rhythms burrowed into their ears and their thoughts. The tassels were made of two different materials, each having their own weight and shine, and moved at irregular speeds, tangling and untangling themselves. The swirling motion became hypnotic and as they watched, it began to warp and skew their sight. Nihal's vision began to grow blurry, and he tried to regain his focus by squinting. Leah, too, had lost a little consciousness and was adjusting her head to the left, to the right, crunching her face and trying to attain a clear view again. As the snake-like tassels mingled with the wind the sky before them became like a kaleidoscope, rolling clouds of different shape and colour appeared before them, swirling and merging with orbs of light, the snakes began to lengthen. Defying gravity they grew outwards and up into the sky, like a tree uprooted and hung upside down with all its soil falling to the ground like rain. *"Aha! Here we have it! I've got something!"* Womblot jumped to his feet and placed both hands firmly on the cane which began to bend and buckle under the stress of the extreme changes taking place before them. *"Now I've got you!"* Womblot spoke through a clenched jaw as he used all his strength to wrestle with the mighty sky. Both Leah and

Nihal had departed into a semi-hypnotic state, Womblot's rhythms and whatever he had plucked from the wind was hypnotising them intensely.

Abstract and inconsistent, a predominant colour of green or black could be seen, many types of tree, wood and forests growing. A wandering man and a woman, marching men, smoke billowing and ravens circling like the swirling of a galaxy. Leah's head rolled around uncontrollably in unison with the mystery before them. Nihal's eyelids flickered rapidly, mesmerised - they were both in a state of dreaming. *"Now! You, Ahhhh!"* Womblot struggled to hold onto his cane and he rolled around on the ground as the wind tried to take it from him .*"No you don't! I've got you, Ara-you-catch!"* he shouted. Leaning back, he dug the cane's end into the ground for support and levered it towards him - *"Aha I've got you this time!"* he said. His heels buried themselves into an area of moss covered soil and the wood began to crack and splinter under the great strain. *"Haha! Not this time Arackach, I've got you!"* Womblot held stiff and gave a firm tug and then snap! The snakes transformed back into tassel's and flung themselves back into his face. The wind fell silent, tearing the sky from its dramatic state. All at once a tranquillity collapsed itself onto the mountain top.

Nihal and Leah came to attention. Their eyes were possessed, bulging brightly, white with inspiration and life. Neither were clear on what had just happened, but both now knew what was next. *"Scattercorn!"* they said together, enthusiastically jumping to their feet. Looking at each other and over their shoulders, they saw Womblot sat on the ground cross-legged, moss and soil all over his face, in his hat and pockets and in his hair, muddied from his struggle he sat with his neck bent forwards, mumbling into the ground. On his lap was his now cracked and bent cane and only half as many tassels as there had been before. *"I almost had it. Damn drat you, Arackach. I almost had you. My rod, damn it. You broke it."* He looked up at them both, *"Did you see it? Did you find him or you or any clue?"* he asked. Leah spoke up with enthusiasm, *"Yes, I saw Scattercorn, we saw Scattercorn! Marching men! Black birds and smoke."* Leah indicated what she saw with her arms spread outwards. Inspired, she got to her feet and re-created the scene, and Nihal acted out all that she said, assuming a straight body for a forest and a stamping march for men. *"Oh, you did, how wonderful. Well done! Then you know what comes after two?"* a once again enthusiastic Womblot asked. Not entirely sure of the question, and expecting another of Womblot's riddles, Leah spoke timidly *"One?"*. Womblot jumped up, *"Correct! You are improving! Excellent work you two. Now, follow on I'll show you where you can see the tree with she and he"* he strutted off towards the lower shelf of Arackach. The eastern side was drenched in sun throughout the day, it was draped in a wonderful quilt of grass that rippled in the breeze like an ocean, a splendid example of untouched natural beauty. Streams ran through it like veins on a leaf, and pink granite and salt bricks flanked the waters' path. Dotted amongst the other features, it was all but freckles on a young girl's face.

"Let's all move a little lower before night falls. My friends, I will set you off in the right direction. Follow on, the water moves quickly, it knows the quickest way down" Womblot skipped on ahead over large grey slates that lay amongst the grass and granite that had been arranged by wear and tear and time and nothing more, yet grouped together like flocking birds in flight, sporadic yet ordered. The three moved down the mountain and a little time passed by.

As they were walking down, Womblot stopped and pointed into a small pool that had been formed in the nearby stream's meander. *"Look here! It's thick, come quick!"* he rhymed as Nihal and Leah skipped over to him. *"You see here the eyes of Arrack, the colour of stone and layers of life,"* Womblot continued, casting his open palm across the water's still surface, clogged with algae, twig and grass, which ignored the clear flowing of the stream that birthed it. *"It looks like mud soup to me"* said Nihal, Leah giggled into her sleeve. Womblot indicated something to the water with his hand and it rippled spontaneously, arranging its mucky surface into an organised fractal structure. *"Look! Look how it orders itself alone and together. There is no other matter of life than that which occurs from strife"* he spoke in his usual rhyming rhythm. The two friends listened as keenly as always making sense of what they could. In time, Womblot insisted - they would indeed make sense of more than they could imagine.

The night arrived. It was black and it was clear. The clouds that had bellowed in the day settled down with the sun and now a yellowy grey half moon hung above the land. *"Look down at the town below, see how it gathers itself, just as does all else,"* Womblot said pointing into the night and towards the twinkling glows of Redchop. The lights of street and building sparkled in the night, a constellation reflecting the stars above. Womblot's hand ventured behind his back and pulled from his satchel, a smoking pipe. He cleaned it with his thumb and blazer and lit a match.

Puffing away he continued *"Look how they organise themselves without realising, the land is the skies and they do not know it. The sky's they argue a certain pattern and we on earth are passed the baton. All things but same and nothing escapes, that which is he and she in the lakes. In the wind, in the planets and the sun, there is of course, only one!"* Womblot chanted in his special way.

The friends had gotten better at understanding Womblot and could see what he referred to. The town of Redchop had organised itself like a constellation of stars. Grouped in places and spread out in others, it both sprawled and coagulated at times just like the mud soup in the stream. All that appeared was of its own free will, Redchop had grown like any other form of life. The town of Redchop's arrangement had not been planned with ruler and grid like those modern cities and towns. It had stood there for very many centuries, had had many people come and go and grown in a natural way over this time, houses and shops stacked upon each other one or two, and sometimes more at a time in often what seemed an illogical fashion. *"You see it's all around us, that which before and before which that's, do not hesitate, just throw your rod and weave your thatch,"* Womblot said, and he whipped his bent cane back behind his head and returned it out over into the night sky where its remaining tassels mingled freely with the stars. *"You see it all occurs on its own without moan, there is no reason for us to groan, or applause that which is foretold, we are just observers, all or most, young and old,"* Womblot said and stood up. *"You will both see this all around your house forever. So, get used to it!!"* he finished in a conclusive tone. Spreading his arms in celebration of that which he'd shared and loved *"Ah! Womblotian"* he exclaimed, embracing their surroundings with smoky breath and satisfaction.

The night carried on this way for some time and they both listened intently, absorbing the meaning behind Womblot's words which were now well understood. He made clear to them the order that surrounds the mountain, how there is draught and wind and chaos, yet all sits evenly and docile under the night sky, which itself appears to them calm but is full of fire and flame, creation, chaos and destruction. The two friends were learning about the world in a way most peculiar to what they were used to back home in school. Nothing felt organised or structured. All had been, and continued to be, unpredictable - lots of fun and at times extremely confusing.

Womblot could sense that his friends needed to rest and began suddenly, *"We can all sleep here tonight,"* he said. Pulling out a tiny folded rug from his satchel he cast it out before them. It unrolled itself suspended in the air without assistance, to a size much larger than expected, and it floated onto the ground peacefully. *"Perfect,"* he said and indicated with his arms in his usual way that this was indeed a perfect place to sleep. *"Don't worry friends, you are safe here on Arackach, nothing of wrongdoing will ever come to Womblotian. Oh oops..."* Womblot dashed over to his cane still swirling in the early midnight air and pulled it in, checking the end of the tassels, twisting them with his fingertips *"Drat it! I almost had something again, missed another one,"* he muttered. *"What is that?"* asked Leah looking at the mysterious cane. *"Have I not explained?"* started Womblot. *"This is a special drail wood mountain rod, I made it myself. This is my aerial, so to speak, it moves with the winds and shows paths that can't be seen through clear air. Think of the feather, it floats and wobbles as it travels, it can demonstrate the wind's decisions to all that look, but what else is there behind its movements? Could you see the movement without the feather? Through my cane I can watch the spirits of the sky as they travel down the mountain side. This was where I first saw you both before you came here,"* Womblot said and smiled as he suggested he had seen their dreams and the wind that brought them.

"You mean, the dream I had at home about the spring - you saw it too, from up here?" Nihal blurted out with amazement. *"Hummm. Well,"* Womblot chirped, *"up here, you can see everything, haven't we already proven that!?"* He smiled his usual smile and stopped for a moment, and his face changed to one more thoughtful, He started again on a different train of thought, *"Oh, ah. Maybe not, maybe I missed something,"* he said, and he looked up and around - he seemed to be talking or listening to something. *"Ok. Understood,"* he whispered over his shoulder. *"Come on you two, let's go on a bit further and stop closer to the wood of Scattercorn."* Womblot's rug sprang up and squirrelled itself back into the satchel. He smiled at the friends, his teeth a charming glint in the moonlight. *"Come on now children, not much further."* Womblot kicked out in front and stepped off towards the dark forest of Scattercorn that began lower down the mountainside.

Decisions Clearing

The three walked on together entering the outskirts of the woods of Scattercorn. Nihal and Leah were both quite tired. Womblot led by a few metres and although quieter than usual, he was not tired in the slightest. He sprang from ball of foot to toe to heel, spinning his rhymes whilst walking, dancing with each step, keeping himself comforted, energised and entertained. Up ahead, Leah could see a sharp beam of moonlight cutting through the concave forest ceiling as the web of leaves and branches of the canopy thinned. Ahead, they could see rows and rows of black minarets bolting up out of the ground like monuments to some forgotten and forsaken activity. *"What is this, Womblot, what are those things? Statues?"* Leah asked, yawning, as she pulled at one of his sleeves. *"No, no no, not statues, they are tree stumps chopped down in olden times by Men of Old. The Trees of Decision. The plinths of change - if I remember correctly,"* Womblot said, flicking through a small booklet he had just pulled from his satchel. *"Yes, ehem. Here we are."* He cleared his throat, lit a candle, and placed it on the tip of his hat. An orange glow shared his immediate proximity. He began to speak, reading from the booklet.

"Decisions Clearing, a place in Scattercorn left in loving and bitter memory of those who have lived, those who will live again, and those who never lived at all." Womblot's eyebrows lifted and his lips pouted with this little confusion. He flicked through the pages on either side

to double check he had not missed anything and found they were blank. "*Oh, that appears to be all. There is nothing more,*" then, folding back a page he read again, "*Decisions Clearing, a place in Scattercorn left in loving and bitter memory of those who have lived, those who will live again, and those who never lived at all... Interesting...*" he proclaimed, nodding his head and rubbing his stubbly chin. "*Wouldn't you say - my friends?*" he smiled. Leah and Nihal were tired and didn't really follow what Womblot had just read nor his question on the matter. They looked at each other. "*We don't understand,*" they said together, too weary to think it through at all.

"*Aha! of course you don't understand,*" Womblot piped up with his characteristic unpredictable energy. "*That's why we are here, my dear dears, we didn't share the wind for fear but for here. You must stay a night to understand. Ha! That's why we came, nothing happens by accident in Womblotian, haven't we discussed this? With this or that we made a hat and on the back there was a map - it was in our dreams now in your head - we came here to bring it out and lay it... dead!*" Womblot finished and did a little twirl, his excitement bubbling over. "*I shall now walk you both the last of the short distance ahead, we will find you somewhere nice and pleasant and safe to sleep and by tomorrow, you will have seen all you need and filled your bellies. Doesn't that sound reasonable?*" he jiggled, beaming with enthusiasm as some molten candle wax dripped onto his nose. "*Ouch! Damn it who put that there!?*" Womblot flinched and swatted the candle from his hat like a pestering insect. *"Stupid thing!"* The two friends managed to giggle a little through their tiredness, Womblot's disposition was joyously infectious. *"I guess that does sound okay"* said Leah, optimistic but sleepy. *"Good! Glad to see you both so excited! Now let's go. Two more minutes!"* Womblot finished and off they went.

Womblot led the way forwards into the centre of the clearing. *"It's a little creepy here"* whispered Nihal to Leah as he looked around at the mushrooms and spider webs that cast menacing silhouettes, shadowy nets in the moonlight. Womblot stopped and spoke up. *"OK, here will do nicely! So, you can sleep here. There is your bed."* Pointing to the left, he showed them a pile of bark, fern frond and rags. Something sparkled amongst the knotted mess. *"It's not as nice as my rug but this bark is very comfortable, it's soft and warm. Don't mind the mites they only eat wood, so you'll be fine"* he said. Nihal and Leah glanced at one another nervously, not fully believing Womblot's reassurances , but they were tired, they could sleep pretty much anywhere. *"What are these things here?"* they thought, noticing a sparkling at their feet.

Looking closer, Nihal realised the glinting from the twisted pile of debris was in fact the shine of polished metal. Some crystal glasses, new and glistening and decorated with precious metals, lay partly buried in the heap. *"Where are these from? I don't see any place for a drink,"* Nihal asked as he stared at the glasses at their feet. *"Oh, they are here from years ago, when this place was being built by Men of Old. The same men who chopped down those trees. Don't worry, only the odd snail there now,"* said Womblot and he kicked one of the glasses to prove his point. Some bubbling liquid dribbled out, still frothing as though fresh. Womblot made no issue of this but it caught Leah's eye. *"OK little ones, I am now done on my piece of your journey, I will go back to my hill... OK, sorry Sir!"* and he had looked over his shoulder as though being corrected by an authority *"back to my Mountain, I mean... and there I shall continue my observations. It was a pleasure to have met you both and I hope the times ahead prove to be as splendid and as varied as they have been up to now. From me, him, and all Womblotian - It is Good Night!"* Womblot spun on his heel and stepped backwards. Before Leah and Nihal had a chance to say a word, he was gone. Womblot disappeared into the night without trail or track, gone as though he never even existed beyond their young eyes.

"OK, Leah, what is this place? I would rather have slept on the mountain to be honest, it was nicer there. I didn't understand Womblot's explanation and it's creepy here" Nihal said, he sulkily kicked the bark on the ground and poked his friend in the shoulder as she bent forward to pick up one of the glasses. *"It smells like champagne,"* Leah said, sniffing the liquid. *"Oh, now that would be nice now wouldn't it, my dad had gotten some bottles of Scattle."* Nihal replied talking fondly of home. Leah took a small sip and passed

it to Nihal, "*Here Nihal, it tastes OK.*" Nihal took the glass and had a small sip. As he tried to speak his voice dropped off into silence - his lips moved but without any sound to follow. Instead, out of the distance the sound of drums rolled and rumbled into the clearing.

Deep drums drummed. Shouting and laughter bellowed up, all at once an armed battalion of noise arose seemingly from out of nowhere, out of the forest, out the night, shouting and arguing suddenly, it was like a drunken wedding from back home. The two were startled and scared yet a cold stillness controlled their reactions. Their wrists were bound with invisible leather and their arms moved underwater. The words they attempted to utter were trapped behind teeth that were clenched. With twisted jaws, their words remained unspoken and caused havoc in their minds as the night air swelled with an ambience that slowed time - it was paralysis, at least for them. The noise was now so strong it pressed into the crowns of their heads, a swelling headache and nausea flooded their psyche, the fluid in their skulls pulsating a hypnotic rhythm that brought with it hallucinations. Nothing had moved or changed around them, only the incredible and deafening drums drumming, thumping inside their skulls.

"They all collapse around me as I am the one. I am here for my God, not for you! I am to conquer and destroy, an entity of unrelenting power and fury! I am here to possess you. Everything is mine at birth, there is nothing I should take from society - it is all mine in the first

instance! I just go and I pick it up, the repossessed. I will do as I choose and as I am instructed to do so by the creator. 'Give what thy shall and take what thy please' - that's what I say, and all you who have courage know it is true! I Arthrues, hammered out on the anvil with fire and flame and a smoke that blackens all who come close enough to observe.

I am Arthrues Arothor! And I am unforgiving!

Who is with me?"

A strong and vengeful voice bellowed out from nowhere, and the words gathered with it a rowdy cheer from the dark forest. Bats hurled themselves from the trees where they hung, clustered in the sky like a grey and black smog, darker and more harrowing than a plagued and dying child. The noise and fear was such that a little blood trickled from Nihal's perforated eardrums, his insides were shaken and his guts were in disarray.

Another voice raged:

"Attention! Get down from there you disgusting brute! Disgrace of a man you are - you have no soul and no courage for yourself. You cry and scream to be joined by the courageous, but you preach the words of a coward. Why would one so strong seek to conquer, exact revenge

and take if he already is in such a lofty position, consulting with God as you do claim? You are not a man, Arthrues!

You are not one of us! You are not welcome here!"

The shouting ended and was replaced with a chatter similar to the kind of bickering found at dinner parties, a twitter more relaxed and less potent than the exaltation and vaunt that had preceded it moments ago. The voices grew in variety and tone, they considered things between them, and wine glasses clinked. The two friends were as scared as they had ever been. Were they dreaming again? This time they actually hoped so.

"Can I just say? Everything is okay ." A small delicate voice offered itself to the conversation.

"Quieten down, child," another older and gruff voice hastily stamped it out.

"Evil, the selfless act. By Arthrues Arothor, " a youthful, clean shaven, angular, and strong looking man spoke up in a rough but charming tone.

"*Quiet now, please. Quieten down now, everyone!*" the mediator spoke. The shallow drums and the bickering fell flat to allow Arthrues Arothor his time to speak.

The two friends recognised the name 'Arthrues' but they couldn't think where from. They tried to look upwards but their petrified necks were too stiff to move. They rolled their eyes upwards towards their foreheads, even having to tilt their heads all the way back to see the huge men standing up upon black tree stumps, proud as the monuments they were. The trees Womblot had said were chopped down by men, were these the same men? they thought. The men stood like towers in the night. With straight backs, firm, tall and lofty, they faced one another like characters carved for life on the chess board. Some were strong and statuesque, some were old and some were young, but all were resolute in their purpose. The sweat of man in all his incarnations swelled in the night air, and a warm glow appeared to lift the earth beneath by a foot or two casting a ripple into the surroundings.

"*Ehem*" spoke Arthrues Arothor, clearing his throat first.

"*The only thing one must do, is die. All else is a choice. Death is the default end of all existence. Unavoidable, inescapable. Death can only be postponed and deferred by the choices of life.*"

After Arthrues made his statement, all number of cheers and jeers rang out in both agreement and disapproval. Flowers and stones were thrown at the man talking. Shoes, branches, glasses of champagne - anything that was at hand was flung towards the speaker and rained above the friends like loose arrows of mediaeval warfare. The debris hit the ground with crashes and thuds at Nihal and Leah's feet, but nothing ever touched the two. Trapped in their bodies and denied expression of any kind, they had no choice but to endure this flogging. Arthrues Arothor continued,

"*Therefore, all creations occur from the fear of death and by extension death itself. They are the product of desire to prolong and preserve life and escape death. Society itself is the aggregated result of this fear and the postponing of the inevitable. Humans have created it as such, to distract and protect themselves from that which they all absolutely and unavoidably face. Death. Society is escapism. Were it not for society, the earth would soon turn them all back into soil for its own selfish purposes.*"

Initial fears, as men, were the uncertainty of the weather, fear of the beasts of the earth and this gave rise to textiles, housing, farming, and then as we feared one another, to weaponry. And here we are today now Gentlemen, we moved on to the modern world and all up to this point was created by fear - yet - all this is functioning to do good, and make life easier for those that live today - wouldn't you agree?"

There was muttering from the crowd as the men considered the words of Arthrues Arothor. *"Please continue Arthrues,"* encouraged the mediator.

Arthrues continued*"So then Gentleman, can we say that fear is making our lives easier? And death too?"*

Laughter broke out amongst a small group and one man heckled*"Arthrues is insane!"*

"You may laugh Gentleman. You may call me insane but where would we be, I ask you, without death? Without the fear of it? What about more tangible examples like pain? Gentleman, do you like pain?" Arthrues Arothor asked the audience.

"What about evil?" A voice interrupted from the crowd.

Arthrues Arothor continued *"Yes, what about evil? Those that are cruel, and those that are evil create fear amongst men, is this not the case? And this then feeds the fearful mind to seek an alternative, does it not? In a broad sense, Gentleman, I argue that this is the metaphysical and ethical representation of the mathematical double negative where, in fact, two wrongs can indeed make a right. And so we conclude! The creator of fear and evil in men, is paradoxically, the embryonic creator of all that is "good" and the prolonger of life for the many. I offer you this Gentleman! Society owes a great debt to those who do evil and those who create fear. What say you all!?"*

"Very interesting, Arthrues" confirmed a number of the men. An old man with a long beard and long white robes began,

"Men, you all know me, I am Arthrues. I have been part of the clearing for many centuries. What is being discussed by our esteemed colleague contradicts profoundly conventional spiritual and religious teaching - that being that it is evil that must be banished for good to prosper amongst men. We have heard the claim this evening that evil and fear are beneficial for life because a lack thereof means the lack of a catalysing good. What would follow if there were no fear? Perhaps the inevitable destruction of man? Perhaps the premature decay and death of a society or species?"

Objections rose in the night and all manner of things were again hurled at the Men whose theories were very unpopular. Arthrues Arothor had finished speaking, and he lowered his arms and dropped the crumpled piece of paper he had been reading from, as if it would never be needed again. Then he gave a graceful bow and the crowd fell silent on this command as though a curtain had been drawn across a stage. At that moment the commotion withered away, leaving no memories of what had been said at all.

"Dear Gentleman, Sirs! Let us all thank Mr Arothor for his contribution to the clearing this evening." The voice of the mediator again commented, *"and let's move on to the next speaker, which I have down as a Mr Arthrues Arothor"* he finished.

"Well, Arthrues, this feeds directly into my argument from a few months prior our congress this evening" Another man of similar age to the first, but a little less muscular and chiselled spoke up in a relaxed voice. The attention of the crowd immediately recognised the new participant and, in a military-like manner, bolted left to face him in unison and salute as if soldiers on parade.

"The argument, if you do recall" he continued, *"was that the fearless are the do-nothings. They sit around and create nothing for they do not fear death and nor do they try to escape it. Why would they need to do anything at all after resigning themselves to this reality? It is the*

fearful that run around like maniacs in search of something to hold and keep inside. They spend their lives jumping through hoops in a vain attempt to save their soul. All that exists in Redchop and beyond was made by those that fear something, pain, death, or even worse, life itself - some are so fearful of life that they focus solely on death – and how to avoid it. What a splendid paradox!"

Arthreus finished speaking. "*Misery seeks much company,*" heckled members of the crowd expressing amusement before being abruptly silenced by the mediator. Whether it was the content or the delivery of the previous speech, the two friends couldn't really tell, but the crowd were now acting in a muter tone. Without introduction, a voice older than those heard before began to speak.

"We are not here to ask who is right, who is good or who is evil. We are here to allow all things to transpire, allow all to continue without victory ever being acquired by any one camp. We must not directly interfere with activities of one group of society, but only encourage and facilitate all actions, creative and or destructive. It is through that oscillating disparity and chaos, that harmony truly emerges. We as wise men must not interfere with those that push the extreme in either direction, for it is they that sacrifice themselves in the process. We must not fear, ever fear, the outcome of what they do. To think without fear is to be free and we are chosen as the guardians of change, this is why we are here – to guard Decisions Clearing!"

A young man spoke up.

"Arthrues! You are right! With regard to your points on religious dogma. We must consider deeply the teachings of the religions and God. If there is a just God and if God is good as all religions do profess, then why!? May I ask does mankind encounter suffering and misery?! And why the Devil? There! There is the answer!"

"What do you mean, Arthrues?" responded all in the clearing in chorus.

Arthreus addressed the clearing *"God has created the Devil to act upon men so they can respond with goodness and with beauty in the physical world. God is too beautiful and magnificent to be fathomed by men. God is incomprehensible within the mortal world and with the limitations of the five senses and thus, the Devil is created by God - as a more primitive structure than he - a structure that is capable of existence on earth, in the mortal realm, to encourage and provoke, to catalyse, mankind to act in the right way and do God's work, in this world, in this domain of this Earth! Where he cannot exist!"*

Cheers erupted from the crowd. *"Arthrues, that is an excellent theory my friend!"* responded Arthrues Arothor and there was a *"Here here"* from the clearing in agreement.

"Gentleman, Gentleman! Arthrues, allow me to contribute! If I may. My name is Arthrues, you know me well as the son of Arthrues and grandson of Arthrues. Two great men of honour who contributed more to this clearing than all of you combined! What we have identified here is the existence of multiple domains that overlap one another, spheres within spheres within spheres If you will."

Arthrues, son of Arthrues and grandson of Arthrues, snapped his fingers and at that moment, glasses appeared in the hands of all the men in the clearing, delicate glasses, gilded with precious metals, such as the ones Leah had picked up from the forest floor. It started to rain. Huge droplets like glowing pearls fell from the sky. The men in the clearing all at once turned their heads upwards and became frozen like statues. The rain fell and in a mere few seconds their glasses were filled with this glowing liquid. The men all raised their glasses ready to drink together. *"Gentleman, Gentleman, I propose a toast to the great man, Arthrues,"* said Arthrues Arothor with celebration from the Clearing. All the men drank together, emptying their glasses with a single gulp.

"What is the point of all this?" a small voice spoke up from the far end of the clearing. A little boy stood there on a box on top of one of the tree stumps so that he came close to the height of the others. *"Maybe things are OK as they are and do not need to be discussed every night.*

Why do we need to always be arguing about that which can never be resolved?" he asked the clearing. Bellows of mocking laughter and disapproval erupted from the men. A condescending tone prevailed and at that moment Leah and Nihal were freed from their paralysis and seized the opportunity to run free. *"Foolish child of Arthrues,"* the oldest of the bearded men spoke up. *"Foolish you are, boy. If everything were as well as you say, and there was indeed no point to any of this - then what would be the purpose of our wisdom - and what would happen to the Clearing?!"*

The Man in the Woods

The two friends woke up in a bundle under a small tree from which hung hundreds of white and downy flowers. They were both covered in this downy cotton-like material and began to rub and scratch as soon as they woke. The debates of the Clearing had lay siege to their minds, and all previous learning from parent and teacher had been thrown into question. They both had a headache. *"My head hurts. Perhaps from the drink?"* Nihal asked. This part of Scattercorn was many miles higher than sea level and the atmosphere was thin enough to let through more sun than normal. The morning warmed quickly! They had no real memory of how they had gotten to this spot or how they had escaped the clearing and its wretched, forsaken philosophies. It must have rained overnight. The soaked wood of the forest was now a polished black, glistening under the bright sun. Shiny black bark, haunting and beautiful all at once. The trees of Scattercorn stood like an army of soldiers assuming various formations, decorated with white and pink budding, delicate green shoots and white blossoms, regalia like a flowering nobility.

"Well, there's no more messing around now! Since Womblot left this is not much fun, I want to go home. I was scared last night Leah" said Nihal, in a bit of a panicked strop. The Clearing had upset him. It had shaken him in places that didn't need attention. *"Leah,"* he began again, *"it's becoming too dangerous and pointless now. The spring is*

here – so what's the point in going any further?" Picking at a small sapling he continued, *"There is no reason to be here. I need to get back. I have to work! My dad, he will be worried and angry if I'm not there to help with the equipment for the fields. I don't want to make him angry. Let's go back!"* Nihal's father drank a lot. He was a stern man of the fields who had little interest in his son being anything other than a farm hand. It was something Nihal dealt with in his own way. Usually by assuming a simple and happy role amongst the family, and this gave him the skills necessary to defuse the complications which inevitably occur between people. Nihal's abundance of generosity meant he was often taken for granted. Leah was as guilty of this as others, but she did share herself with Nihal, too, or so she felt. She felt like it was her that was leading and making the hard choices, like she was the one responsible for them both. It was a peculiar mix that both, even as closest of friends, sometimes misunderstood.

"Nihal! There is no way back that way. Can't you remember how we got here? In the night and with Womblot from the top of the mountain! It's not going to work if we go up again, why are you being like this?" Leah's tone was harsh and sour. Nihal's face dropped. He didn't want to fight, he fell silent. *"Nihal, I don't know that we can just turn back. Where and which way would we go? I think the only way now is to move south through Scattercorn until we hit the plains again and we can then find a road that would lead us back home."* Leah didn't want to turn back but neither did she wish to encounter the madness of the

clearing again, the memory of it was delirious and nonsensical. The events of their journey had begun to make an impression on them, in more ways than one.

They moved on and the forest thickened. Large trees grew in number and the smaller were crowded out, suffocated and deprived of life by the great and the strong. "*What were those men talking about Leah? It was scary,*" Nihal asked, trying to strike up a conversation in order to end the difficult silence between them. "*I have no idea. Womblot said it would provide us an answer, but I don't know what that could have been. It wasn't much fun at all,*" responded Leah.

A short way in front, Nihal could see a tower of smoke puffing gently upwards into the forest canopy and forming a small wispy cloud beneath the treetops. Circled by ravens, which sculpted the cloud into all matter of shapes, the cloud shifted and danced as if it was alive. Nihal looked down into the thatched forest floor and picked up a small stick. Trying to be quiet he threw it in Leah's direction who was at this point, several paces ahead. As it tumbled through the air, the cloud turned towards them and the ravens changed course. The stick landed squarely on Leah's nose, "*Hey!*" shouted Leah, loud enough for her voice to scatter some of the local dragonflies, "*why did you do that?*" Nihal raised his eyebrows and looked to the left, "*Leah, be quiet, there is a camp up ahead,*" he announced. "*But we're in Scattercorn, there aren't any people here,*" said Leah. "*Well, look!*" Nihal's fingers left his baggy sleeve to point at the smoke that was now stretching itself towards them, like an arrow pointing straight at its target - the ravens had swooped in their direction dragging the smoke with them.

Glancing up and ahead, Leah could now see it, too. *"Oh, we should be quiet, we don't want any unwanted attention, Nihal."* Rolling his eyes for a second time Nihal moved on in the direction of the smoke. *"Let's see if it's safe,"* he said, crouching into a more stealthy posture as they moved. Not wishing to repeat the encounter of the clearing, they both moved cautiously onwards together, parting branches gently with their arms so as not to disturb the forest and make any noise. Scattercorn was dry here and twigs underfoot would split and pop gently with a small puff of dust, thus making being quiet rather difficult.

Having moved a few metres closer, the two friends could see up ahead between two folded trees, a short man hunched over a long cane, a knobbly cane made of the same drail wood that Womblot had carried. It was twice as long as the man and he held it mid-way. Drail wood was known back home for its straight branches and was popular with arrow makers but very rare and very expensive. They were not used to seeing it this often.

The man wore a beard between his ears, chin, and knees. Practically covering his whole torso, this long and greyed beard had collected debris from the forest floor as he wandered around. It was filled with flowers, twigs and acorns and dry leaves, and possibly a mouse or two. The man looked up slowly in the direction of the two friends. Nihal was a little in front but only by a few steps, he looked back and Leah looked with eyes wide and startled. The man stood casually, as if he had known they were there all along, just waiting patiently outside for them, waiting for them to pluck up enough courage to approach him. *"Leah, what shall we do?"* whispered Nihal over his shoulder as Leah crouched a few steps behind him. *"Well he's seen us now, hasn't he. He doesn't look dangerous, and he seems to be alone. Let's go and speak to him and introduce ourselves. We should apologise for intruding and tell him why we are here. Maybe he knows the winds like Womblot did. Maybe he can tell us about the Clearing, he lives here after all,"* said Leah and Nihal nodded in approval. The two stood up straight, deciding it was no longer necessary to hide. They composed themselves and walked briskly towards the old man who was now smiling hospitably. Like two tourists in a foreign land, they were no threat to him.

From a distance, the man spoke with a slow, gruff, seemingly unpractised voice, *"Come forth, I can see you, why do you hide?"* The man's voice creaked like an old tree in the wind. *"Come on closer now,"* he said. Nihal and Leah both continued to walk confidently towards the old man, and as they got closer, he seemed to be even more hunched over and frail than before. Feeling less threatened, they spoke ahead as they walked towards him. *"Dear Sir, we are travelling through, that is all"* Nihal said, proud of himself, the best greeting he could muster. *"We are from Redchop,"* said Leah, waving sweetly. The man's head remained still behind his hood, only his shiny green eyes acknowledged that he had heard them speak. The two were now within throwing distance of the man and feeling very happy with their approach. *"He seems harmless,"* Leah whispered quietly.

His voice bellowed, *"It is not life that I seek, my youthful followers"* and his head jolted forward to face the two friends. They stopped dead in surprise at his sudden speed and vitality *"It is blood!"* he concluded with venom. His eyebrows rolled down towards his nose, crinkling the skin between his brow to suddenly achieve a rather menacing glare. Nihal and Leah stopped dead; white as ghosts, they were frozen in shock. They had blindly mistaken this old man as a harmless figure. He did not seem dangerous, he was short and bent, his voice croaky with no ill intent – were they about to relive the clearing?

The old man faced Nihal squarely, his height, shoulders and chest grew as he began to rise from the knees, up past their heads and above the small berry bushes that grew around the forest. The man had been kneeling, his cloak and beard so vast they couldn't tell. He now stood tall, huge like a giant, his drail wood cane in fact only at shoulder height. Leah squirmed inside. She wanted to say something powerful and strong to protect Nihal but she, like him, was shuttered with fear. The two friends found themselves cowering below what they had previously stood above, their confidence gone - now a whitened fear painted their faces. The man's lips peeled apart and they both awaited what would surely be his final words before they were chased away, threatened, captured or hurt. Consumed by fear, their hearts stammered, time slowed in what seemed like their final moment - those isolated, confused heartbeats to be their last. The man's mouth was now wide enough to shout his dreaded phrase, a bellowing rumble began in his lungs and throat and the two friends knew only moments were left for them.

Laughter broke the silence. A big grin then appeared on the old man's face, now almost appearing childish, as he leant forwards and down to be at their height again. *"Only joking!"* he chuckled.

The rush of blood that flowed through Nihal's veins was enough to achieve euphoria, and he promptly fainted. Leah, always more resolute but still shaken by the ordeal stammered *"You are not... You are not going to hurt us?"* she begged. *"Of course I am not, you nitwit,"* exclaimed the man, *"you think I would live out here on my own if I were looking to hurt people? Hurt who? Noone ever comes here. Why do people have these warped views of the loner, I do not know."* The man thrust his hand deep into his huge beard and plucked out a short stick. Skilfully trimming it of imperfections with his long immaculate fingernails he placed it between his lips as a toothpick, and revealed a wonderful set of teeth lined up like pearls.

He smiled once more *"I've been expecting you. Come, pick up your friend, I've prepared for you both a nice refreshing drink."*

The ravens that had been circling above now ended their dance, allowing the smoke cloud to settle down. They scattered and the cloud dispersed, allowing the smoke to rise as it would in a natural fashion, gently puffing its way up towards the forest ceiling once again. The man turned quickly and neatly like a ballet dancer in a strict performance, striding off into his tent with each step in time, brushing aside the large leather sheet that was draped across the entrance. The buzzing vibrations of the crickets now rang loudly from the small grass. Leah looked down to see Nihal still unconscious, his toes wiggling as he lay there in a dream. *"Nihal, wake up,"* Leah prodded with the encouragement of a friendly little kick to his thigh *"Wake up, everything is okay"*. Ever the sound sleeper, Nihal was as usual proving difficult to wake in a conventional fashion, but knowing him as well as she did, Leah bent down and pulled on his big toes as if turning a switch, and Nihal jolted and awoke suddenly. *"I'm okay, I'm okay, it's okay don't worry,"* bleated Nihal, rather dazed. *"Everything is fine, I was just taking a nap,"* he finished. Leah laughed a sweet smile, *"Nihal, you fainted,"* she said with a giggle. Looking from side to side where he sat, Nihal could see his impression squashed into the forest floor, and indeed the earth was flattened in the shape of a small boy laying on his back with arms aside. *"Oh, I can't remember doing that, is everything okay?"* he remarked. *"Yes! Everything is fine now,"* Leah's love for her friend was always clearest at these moments. *"The old man is a friendly man! He played a trick on us and you fainted. But it's okay now, he says he has made us a special drink, he said he knew we were coming. Maybe he is like Womblot. Let's go and sit with him in his tent."* She helped her friend to his feet. Smiling, she brushed him off with firm strokes to his back and legs.

New Shoes

Leah walked in first and parted the opening to the tent with the side of her arm. The leather that hung from the tree above to form an entrance was the thickest she had ever seen, as thick as her thumb, a mighty cow it must have been. Indeed it was so heavy that Leah had to lean forward with all her body weight to even attempt to part the drapes and move inside. "*I need a hand Nihal,*" she said. Nihal leant into her side and between the two of them they were able to make their way through. Parting the drapes and managing their way through the entrance, they were hit by warm air from a stove that sat in the centre of the tent. Hovering over the stove was a pot of steaming liquid, a few items of outdoor clothing and what looked like socks, complete with holes at the heel and toes that were so big, that the sock essentially had no sole. Atop the stove's flat lid was a dark-coloured bread baking in a tin and some herbs. The wonderful smoky aroma made them feel welcome, exciting their nostrils like the spring pollens of Scattercorn.

The old man's tent was cluttered yet somehow organised, looking messy but feeling immaculate. It felt as though not one particle of waste would ever be produced and not a single degree of heat lost from the burning wood. "*Shut the door, will you now,*" spoke the man politely, his voice still deep yet seemingly younger than it had been. He sat at the far side of the tent, cross-legged in a chair made of dried and woven vines, fixed with the same leather as the tent's skin. His left foot bounced at the ankle. *"It's okay, make yourselves at home, sit down and get comfortable, you can be at ease here,"* he said. The man's demeanour had changed to that of a gentleman of fine dialect with a highly cultivated accent. He spoke with a gentle charm, his voice so crisp and spirited it could soothe the angriest oceans. They stepped in and moved confidently towards the warm stove, sitting themselves down on a large bench made of books that had been glued together and finely sculpted at the ends with a chisel. The fire crackled as the wood succumbed to its heat.

"My name is Amsel," spoke the man softly through his beard. *"I live here and have lived here for many years longer than you have breathed, but ultimately we are all here for the same reason,"* he affirmed. Nihal and Leah were both feeling at ease. Amsel's home, voice and relaxed way of being had made a settling impression on them quite quickly. *"I have been here without fellow man for many years. I'm at peace here and as I said outside – why, I ask you - if I wanted to harm others would I live alone here, in the woods?"* he quipped. *"Surely, if I wanted to take from others and extract from them, I would live in your world where there are plenty of souls on offer, plenty of meat at the market."* Leah and Nihal sat mesmerised by Amsel, he spoke so clearly and his wisdom sprawled across the room so that it required no effort to decipher his words unlike the riddles of Womblotian. *"It is a common misconception that those who live alone*

in the forest are of danger to others, a simple mistake learned by those that listen to fools and lies. People that wish to plant their own fear into others. We forest people, few though we are nowadays, are the quietest and most pleasant of folk, can't you see that?" Amsel said. His clean and captivating smile presented itself once more to assure the two that he was correct in his musings, they had had no doubts anyway. *"You two need to be careful with who and what you listen to. The adults of the town Redchop know only themselves and can only see themselves in that which is around them... Now, what would you like to drink?"* he asked and stood up, and with two large steps he had crossed the room in its entirety.

In the corner of the tent sat an old cabinet, this too was constructed of books bonded together with some kind of clear resin and then carved as a solid block. It was decorated with emblems and wildlife, the hinges were made of leather and the handles of wound vine. *"We endured a severe gale a few days back, so I had been expecting you. I prepared a local treat. Of course, when I say local, I mean it's my own special recipe! Local to everything you see and nothing more,"* he smiled, leaning into the cabinet and humming a song, pleased at having the chance to finally share his recipe. *"You know this tonic I made only a few times before. That was for my beloved wife,"* he exclaimed. Twiddling through a few containers that looked to be made of glass, he plucked one out from the back of the cupboard and brushed it off *"Ah! Here we are,"* Amsel said and spun round, thrusting his arm forward holding a jar inscribed with the words "Arackach". *"You were both up on the hill recently, weren't you? Yes, I thought so!"* he smiled.

They both sat quietly, listening to Amsel and enjoying the warm crackling fire. *"I know what happens on Mt Arackach, for I was once there myself. You were taken there by the wind, I presume?"* he asked rhetorically. Nihal gave him a slight nod. Leah tried to confirm with her lips, but before she had a chance to speak, Amsel was again talking. *"It is rather ridiculous this process, I don't know when it will end. Every ten years I seem to live the same story - as if it is planned by him up there,"* and he nodded his head upwards as if to indicate the existence of someone or something high above. *"Here we are yet again, another year and two children from Redchop in my forest and in my tent. Again, following an extremely cold winter..."* He paused and looked at the two friends. *"Maybe it's the winter that pushes man out to find something else?"* he asked with a smile and rummaged through his beard pulling out two wooden bowls which had been carved beautifully. *"Here you are,"* he offered, giving them a vessel each to drink with. Amsel pulled out the leather-bound wooden stopper from the jar with a pop and poured a glowing liquid into the two bowls that were cupped neatly in their hands. *"And here we have it,"* he announced with excitement, *"your first taste of Arackach... You know, my wife left me after she drank this."* The friends' faces dropped. Amsel smiled, *"Only joking,"* he laughed, and he guzzled the liquid straight from the jar. Nihal and Leah looked at one another, they were both thirsty and they both trusted Amsel, but... *"What is.."* began Nihal, *"Don't ask irrelevant questions now, boy"* interrupted Amsel, *"just drink it!"*

The liquid that sat in their bowls glistened like a still winter lake, magnifying the concave grain of the wooden container. As they looked closely, they could see the tree's life within each layer. The liquid bubbled gently and scented their noses in a pleasant way. Their reflections were clearly visible as they stared at the drink Amsel had called Arackach. The liquid mirror showed them looking youthful and healthy, better than they were feeling at least. All the muck and wear from the journey was washed away. They looked at themselves in this liquid and they felt lustrated. Amsel smiled and encouraged them to drink. *"Go on then young ones, don't waste it,"* he prompted.

Nihal and Leah lifted the bowls in unison. The tonic hit their lips and the aroma was a vibrant fervour. The liquid had a flavour much stronger than anything they had ever experienced, impassioning their hearts as it flowed down their throats. A few gulps and it was gone. Amsel beamed with satisfaction in seeing the two cleansed of dirt and grime, their skin shone brightly and they were fatigued no more. *"There, that wasn't so bad now was it?"* he chuckled. Nihal belched, *"It's wonderful Amsel, all my body is dancing,"* he said whilst wiggling his toes. Leah began to hum and whistle a melody, not knowing where it came from - she did so as though it were true.

"Drattt", Amsel ran quickly to the stove, *"I burnt the bread! Why do I always forget about my bread? It sits their next to my socks so I don't forget it and I still manage to forget it every time. Hilda would kill me"* he proclaimed. *"Who is Hilda?"* asked Nihal. *"I thought you lived here alone?"* asked Leah. Amsel picked up his bread tin - *"Ouuuchh!"* he shouted, burning his fingers, he dropped the tin on the floor and the bread fell out neatly. *"Hilda is my wonderful wife, she lives on the other side of Scattercorn,"* he said, picking up the bread and placing it on a wooden board. Nihal and Leah looked at one another confused by this discovery. Not only did Amsel appear too old, youthful, wise and clumsy all at the same time, he was also apparently married. *"Why do you live apart, Amsel, you and Hilda?"* Leah asked. Amsel was sat looking suspiciously at the bread's burnt crust as though it were a conspiracy, *"Every bloomin' time this happens. It always burns,"* he continued under his breath.

"Amsel, why?" repeated Leah. *"Yes! I heard you the first time, dear!"* Amsel said, jumping up and spinning a pirouette in the air like the fine dancer he again - out of nowhere - appeared to be. *"It's simple, she loves me too much! And you, my friend, can go."* He bent over and grabbed the bread with a towel to protect his hands, took one leaping step to the doorway and threw it out into the forest like a sportsman. *"The ravens here love me, too! They are extremely well fed,"* he

smiled, turning back to face them. *"You see, little ones, nothing is ever wasted or lost in life. Everything just changes hands again and again. A simple mistake I continually suffer only leads to the birds being happy. And so, I ask you both, was there ever a mistake made in the first place?"* proclaimed Amsel, essentially talking to himself. In these moments he did not seem particularly interested in any input, only in the opportunity to consider his musings and rhetorical questions out loud. *"You two must be tired after all the walking you have been doing, you need to get some rest before you move on. Take my bed, it is over there in the corner,"* he pointed.

The effects of Amsel's tonic had mostly worn off but they were feeling a warmer and more pleasant type of tiredness than they had been used to the last few weeks. It was the kind of tiredness that you feel after a hearty meal, relaxed and rested, nothing like the moments of exhaustion they had suffered on the way here. Amsel rummaged in his beard and pulled out a huge golden key encrusted with diamonds and gems, it gave them both the impression that it was a key to something important and grand. He spun the key chain on his finger and flicked it off into the air, sending it in the direction of Leah's open and cupped hands. She caught it effortlessly, but as its weight was felt for the first time, her arms fell and her back bent forwards to compensate, the key was surprisingly heavy for something so small. *"That's the key to my room, it's over there, you can sleep as long as you need. I will be outside collecting berries,"* Amsel said and turned in his ever-choreographed fashion. As he left the tent, he brushed aside the curtain that Nihal and Leah had struggled to move between the two of them, he was seemingly incredibly strong, not at all what you would expect from his appearance.

They tiptoed through the tent that seemed to sprawl endlessly now like a labyrinth. As they crossed it step by step, it seemed to expand and go on forever, even time slowed down as they moved. Past the stove and past the carved book bench, they could see in a jumbled pile on the floor many objects, notepads, different types of carving tools, along with half carved utensils, spoons, knives, forks and saucers, all fashioned from drail wood and none of them finished. All the carvings lay within arms distance of the woven basket chair Amsel had first sat down in. It was as if they had just been dropped on the floor there and never revisited.

Together they reached the bedroom door. It was the only door inside the tent to be made of wood and was carved with the usual artwork that they had become used to since arriving. Taking the heavy key with both hands and standing on her tiptoes, Leah managed to place it into the lock which was slightly above her head. She turned the key to the left. With a rusty clunk, the mechanism popped the door ajar and the key vanished into the lock with a woosh. They jumped in surprise and waited, both stood expecting something grand to appear. Given that the key was made of gold and gems it must be the place that

Amsel keeps something of grandeur for himself, they thought. The door gently swung itself open and they stepped into the dark space. *"Where is the light? I can't see much,"* whispered Nihal as if to not disturb the room itself. *"Maybe there isn't one in here,"* responded Leah. *"Do you have a match? Or perhaps grab an ember from the fire."*

A sparkle flashed above them and the key appeared, spinning around, suspended in the air like an orb. A small hole opened in the canopy above, and the sun shone through in a single beam of a yellowish white. The key hung directly in the path of this light, spinning faster and faster, it scattered the rays across the room, illuminating before them a simple wooden bed, large enough for ten or more people. It was both very large and very simple with a hard mattress. The two friends jumped in and lay flat on their backs staring upwards to the spinning orb. Side by side sprawling out from finger to toe their bodies barely occupied a quarter of the bed even as they stretched out. They both gave a sigh of relief. Within seconds they were asleep and the sunlight beamed down onto their toes which twinkled in satisfaction. Some time passed by.

Nihal woke to hear an operatic and poetic singing filling his ears and echoing through the inside of the tent which acted like a large percussion instrument as its sides vibrated. It sounded like Amsel. He gave Leah a poke in the ribs. She woke pleasantly, well rested and feeling wonderful. She stretched her arms, fingers, legs and toes and twisted from side to side to wake her muscles and bones. *"Such a wonderful sleep I had Nihal. I feel wonderful and strong,"* she said, rubbing her eyes. *"Me too yes, me too. I think it's Amsel's magical potion Arackach, I can still feel it warming me,"* Nihal rubbed his belly and smiled happily. The two friends hugged, sharing their happiness between them. The singing continued loudly, *"Let's go and find Amsel and thank him for his kindness,"* suggested Leah.

They both stood up to find shoes upon their feet. A thick leather was wrapped finely around their heels and toes, all corners and contours covered with precision, as though the shoes had been mapped and moulded especially for them. They were stitched finely with an interior seam so that no water could enter and no thorns could tear. A fine example of craftsmanship! *"Ooo, new shoes, new shoes!"* joyed Nihal. *"I've wanted so badly for some shoes since we left Redchop in such a hurry,"* said Nihal, as he danced and stamped around in a jig, throwing his legs and arms out before him. He jumped back onto the bed and shook Leah around, knowing no other way to express his happiness. *"Shoes shoes shoes shoes, new shoes!"* He said with each stamp. Leah was busy inspecting hers in a more mature fashion, commenting on the flawless craftsmanship and artistry. *"Nihal, I have never seen leather like this before. It's so thick and yet it bends without issue and without crease."* She pulled her foot to her nose, *"and oh the smell, the leather must be treated with Scornberries from the forest!*

That's what they smell like!" she said. *"Shoes shoes shoooess!!"* Nihal continued his stamping expressing his jubilation. *"Let's go and thank Amsel!"* they said together.

The two friends ran out into the main room which was now tidy and immaculate. All the clutter that was on the floor had been organised into the baskets hanging from the ceiling, woven sacks dangled above like Halloween lanterns filled with Amsel's eclectic objects and belongings. Remembering that the tent door had been such a task for them to open, they decided to run together and use their motion to assist in moving it - *"Three, two, one- lets go!"* counted Leah, and they both ran straight towards the leather curtain pointing their shoulders towards it as they scrunched their eyes and braced for impact.

At that moment, a gust of wind suddenly picked up and folded the curtain back on itself. The two friends crashed through what was now an open doorway and fell directly into the mound of leaves that the wind had gathered for them outside like a doormat. Laughing, they grabbed handfuls and threw them at one another, rolling around, overcome with happiness they had forgotten all that had brought them to Scattercorn in the first place.

"Hey, look at this tent Nihal. How did all of that fit inside?" questioned Leah. They stood up and stepped a few paces back so as to get a clearer view and perspective of how small the tent appeared to be

from the outside - it was tiny, barely big enough for one small person. Leah walked towards the door to re-examine the tent. Leaning forwards, she took a peek back inside, again showing a large drawn out space. She pulled her head back - just a small tent. *"It's magical!"* proclaimed Nihal *"It's magic! It's Amsel and Arackach and it's new shoes. Shoes shoes shoes!"* He began dancing again and kicking at the piles of leaves as he pranced around.

A raven landed close by and looked at them both curiously with a craned neck, as if they were peculiar in some way. Nihal, still dancing with the leaves, hadn't noticed, but Leah could see that the raven was holding in its beak the great key that had been given to them by Amsel. *"Ohh thank you Mr. Raven. I must return it to Amsel. Where is he, do you know?"* she asked. The raven leapt into the air and thrust out its great wings which sprawled like branches from a black willow tree. It circled them once and disappeared behind the tent. *"Come on, Nihal, let's go and find Amsel and thank him,"* said Leah. Holding hands, they walked around the perimeter of the tent trudging through scrunching leaves. They both sneezed, such was the pollen and haze here as fine dust rose from the leaves underfoot. *"Achoo!"* they both let out in unison. They looked at one another, and then they looked around.

Small white flowers littered the forest floor. All that had previously been a grey or a brown was now shades of green and yellow and red.

The two friends twirled with heads tipped backwards, round and round they span, soaking up the brightly glowing colours. *"Summer is here, so soon!"* said Nihal. They had no idea how long they had been inside Amsel's tent or how long they had slept, but they could see that summer was now blooming lusciously. *"Something in the drink?"* Leah pondered aloud, questioning the passage of time. They plodded on around the tent's perimeter. In just five or ten paces, they arrived at the tent's far side where they had not yet been. There they could see Amsel, slouching in a large tree stump that had been carved appropriately for such a position. It had many different arm rests and bulges, so he didn't have to sit the same way all of the time - upright, slouch, feet up, the chair catered to all of his moods and thought processes. It was coated on one side by fungi and moss on the other, new shoots were poking their way out, the tree stump was not dead. Amsel sat at a wide angle, it was obvious to any observer that serious relaxation was taking place. He had rolled his beard around itself and hollowed it out into the shape of a pot, and they could see it was filled with the berries he had collected.

Amsel sat snacking merrily, flicking berries into his mouth using his thumb. He shared them with the ravens. Amsel would throw them into the air and they would swoop down from the forest canopy. In a single manoeuvre they would catch the berry, eat it, and then spit out the seed which would land neatly in a small pot at the side of the chair. The singing that they had heard when they woke in the tent started again, it had obviously been Amsel.

"

Her smile mesmerised,

Eyes sanctified,

Bleed into the ocean, oh mortal tears,

Bleed so selfishly,

Your love defines your being,

But it must not,

Oh sweet destiny, I love you deeply,

Many years gone and your soul glistens still,

And her eyes, her smile,

Sanctified, mesmerised,

Watching over me,

Forever

"

His poetic singing was interrupted by coughing and choking as he found he couldn't sing, eat berries, and feed birds all at the same time. He leant forward, coughing and spluttering out a large Scornberry stone onto the ground. He picked it up and placed it in the bowl that the ravens were using neatly. Clearing his throat, "*Ehem - aha, my little friends, well rested I trust?*" he asked, smiling again, unphased by his almost choking to death. "*Come and sit with me in my throne will you, I'm going to tell you one more story before you leave to continue on your way. Are you still looking for the spring?*" He smiled, indicating with his eyes and arms thrown out wide that the forest was now clearly a glowing summer. "*Would you like some berries? Here help yourself,*" he offered, placing his beard pot onto one of the chair's armrests so both Nihal and Leah could serve themselves, which they did happily. Amsel continued,

"I was once a dweller in a town similar to your home of Redchop. My mind would ache with over - stimulation. 'The world of problems' was what I would think as a young man. There were so many distractions! So many things were wrong, so much to do and so much to fix that my creative self became overwhelmed and I would jump from one thing to the next, never being satisfied with anything.

There was too much there for me to think about yet there was never a way for me to fix it all. So, I came here, where you can see, all is done so perfectly by the forest. All is correct and beautiful. I don't need to ask any questions or doubt a single thing about what I see here. Such is the omnipotent power of beauty!"

Amsel said, and he threw a Scornberry into his mouth, *"Relax and be happy. Why would anyone want to do anything but relax?"* Amsel finished. *"Well, I like to work and be busy with my things. I like to draw and I like to move and run and play,"* said Nihal *"And I like to read my father's big books and I like to plait my braids,"* seconded Leah. Amsel just smiled and pointed a finger upwards towards the sky whilst talking, and he began again.

"Things just happen, we should relax and just let things happen regardless of the consequence. We will see that history is in fact evidence that things will happen regardless of any idea about what is or should be happening or indeed, what is right. It's wonderfully peculiar. I had a day once in my late twenties, sad and alone after a recent mishap, I looked at the flowers that grew in the back garden of my home. I sat there on a tree stump, not quite as grand a stump as this but a stump of wood none the less. I sat and I looked at the flowers and the blades of grass growing their way and living their life as designed for them. Each one reaching its potential. And I thought, how can these plants grow so beautifully without error, and yet we

people fail so horribly, so many people do not manage to ever bloom? What excuse do we have for this? Is it our design?" Amsel finished on a pause, as though for the first time he was actually invoking an answer from his company. Nihal spoke up *"Well my dad, he thinks too much and that gets him stuck. It would be easier being a dog or cat, he says it all the time. My dad's a farmer."* Amsel smiled a long smile at Nihal. Seeing the youthful truth and bluntness of Nihal's delivery. *"Ah,"* Amsel sighed a deep breath. *"I once had companionship like you both. Before I came here with my wonderful Hilda."* Amsel stopped and re-shuffled himself into a new position, as if changing his thoughts altered his entire being, like a chameleon. His body language was completely different, he now sat more upright.

"So, tell me friends, what do you think it was that brought you here? What's the real reason?" Amsel said with his charming smile looking at them both. He paused briefly and as usual, before he had a reply, he began talking once more. *"You came here to find something, did you not. Something you saw in the wind perhaps?"* and he pointed his finger up without moving his hand from the arm of its chair. A small gust of wind rustled some branches above. *"You followed a strange wind, did you? You left the safety of your homes to find something you were unsure of, and had not questioned whether this was achievable for more than a single breath?"* Amsel went on. *"Yes,"* began Leah, *"we came to look for the spring. The birds had not arrived on time and I became quickly worried. I didn't know what to do so I went to find*

my Nihal who is my best friend." She nudged to the left, *"and he had had the same thing in his dream,"* Nihal piped up, *"Yes, I had a dream and a strong wind was blowing and it took us to the mountain and that was when Leah woke me up but mainly I came because Leah wanted me to,"* Nihal nudged her back.

Leah looked a little guilty and began to reason further with Amsel, *"The wind also blew into the barn and showed us the mountain when we were both awake,"* she said. Amsel peered along his nose at them both like their schoolmaster, a sceptical squint in his eyes and lips curled inwards. *"And tell me, now that you look back at this, does any of this make sense or seem like a good idea?"* Amsel broke out in bellowing laughter and both Leah and Nihal felt a little embarrassed. *"Friends, you have followed a path you chose on a whim, and now you will follow it until the end, I'm sure!"* Amsel said and sat back returning to his relaxed posture. He tossed another Scornberry into his mouth and flicked his foot in the air. Nihal and Leah looked at one another.

The ravens above circled a few times and then scattered, breaking formation and flying off in packs of two and threes. One lone raven swooped down holding a folded piece of paper in its mouth. It flew close to Leah and hovered in front of her, dropping the paper into her cupped hands. The raven squared and then flew off into the east. *"What's this?"* asked Leah. *"It's one of my poems, the ravens collect them. I don't know where they hide them because I rarely get them back,"* said Amsel. *"You can keep that one,"* he smiled. Amsel pointed to one of the ravens that was flying alone. *"There you are my friends,"* tossing another berry in his mouth, *"perhaps the raven wishes for you to follow him."* The raven flew off into the distance, *"And remember as you go, if you shine so brightly that you hurt others,"* Amsel paused with a charming smile, *"just keep shining."*

The woman in the woods

Amsel waved them off in a merry way, shaking his hand from his wrist it fluttered backwards and forwards flamboyantly. *"Take care little ones, take care now won't you? If you see my wife, tell her I said hello,"* Amsel called out. *"Wow what an experience that was, Leah. Amsel was so wonderful and funny. I am very glad that we bumped into him,"* Nihal said. *"Me too Nihal, he is a lovely man and I will tell my mother about him!"* Leah said. They both looked down at their feet, now cosily wrapped within the walls of the leather shoes that Amsel provided them with – walking now felt so much lighter! The forest here was littered with Bluetusk, a small flower with blue petals and white pinstripes which looked rather suave. They could be found closer to Mt Arackach and also by the side of the road in the farmlands, where the hedgerows ensure that moisture and shade are matched perfectly by shadow and sunlight. These small flowers were popular with dye makers back home because of their rich pigment, but they were scarce. Leah picked one and smelt it. *"Oh they smell wonderful!"* said Leah with joy as she inhaled the flower's scent. Nihal bent down to pick one and he broke its neck cleanly so as not to tear at the rest of the plant. Tenacious as they were, like many a small thing, he knew it would regrow if done this way. *"Here,"* Nihal said and placed the flower into Leah's hair smiling. *"It's for you!"*

They moved onwards for a few days or so. Sleeping only once, the Arackach tonic from Amsel had boosted their vitality and endurance considerably. Not to mention the shoes! They got tired only half as much as they had previously, back when they had first entered Scattercorn. The weather now fully convinced them it was midsummer, and the journey they were on had become very enjoyable. They walked through a new Scattercorn, one rustling with animals, sneezing with pollen and buzzing with bees and butterflies. They ducked through and under branches and scrambled fallen trees, slipping on moss and loose bark. The shoes from Amsel were wonderful and held up to all challenge and test. The leather was thick and without padding, like a pair of clogs, but the resins Amsel had applied softened the leather delicately and it curled around their feet like wet sand. *"Shoes shoes!"* Nihal sang again, *"I love my shoes Leah!"* he said.

A little in the distance they could see, dragged into the undergrowth, the winding of a very small and crooked street. A gravel path sunk into the forest and flanked by hedgerows all well-trimmed, prim, proper and cared for meticulously. A small amount of geometry and organisation emerged from the otherwise chaotic harmony of nature. At the end of the path lay an aged and charming cottage, clad in a fine limestone coat, dotted with red and blue brick mosaic and thatched with perfect yellow grass that did not seem possible to attain here in Scattercorn. It sat humbly amongst the forest not in any way out of place and indeed quite charming.

It was a pleasant sight to see after such a long walk. *"Hey, look here!"* said Leah. *"Do you think it's Amsel's wife? He had said she lived at the other end of Scattercorn and he said no others lived here."* Leah added. *"Well it must be then, maybe she has nice drinks, too!"* Nihal smiled childishly excited by the prospect of some more lazing and another Arackach elixir. They walked towards the entrance of the path. Tucked away in the first bushes to the side of the entrance was a little sign carved from wood, *"Very similar to Amsel's carving isn't it, Nihal"* Leah said stripping off some of the ivy leaves and moss that had attached themselves to it, undisturbed for quite some time. Brushing the flora aside revealed a neatly inscribed block of wood, a plaque, dotted with details of local wildlife, herbs and other elements of the forest. Etched deeply in the centre of the plaque it read "Hilda's House." Nihal read out as simply as it was written, *"Hildas house!"* he said. They looked at each other knowing now that they had found Hilda, the wife of Amsel, and were likely to again be treated to wonderful hospitality. They were excited.

They both stood up and made their way down the path. The gravel crunched as it rolled around their feet. *"Just like being on a pebbly beach!"* said Nihal. The wooden door of the cottage opened without a squeak and as the door swivelled open, out popped a tall and beautifully elegant lady with long fine silver hair that reached her ankles. It was bound tightly at her crown, the hair tied across her head smooth and shiny with a long whip tail and white ribbon. She was wearing a long silk dress without detail or design, simple and clean with only a fine blue trim which washed her body in white. She wore a fiery pink pearl necklace around her neck and white painted fingernails. She stood in the doorway with very little to say in the way of expression. No smile, no wave, no open arms and no bad jokes like that of Amsel. She seemed to be rather unemotional, even cold, very strange considering her elegance, they thought. The two children coming down her garden path warranted no expression at all from the lady, as though it was a regular occurrence for her. They felt as though they were about to be turned back like unwanted mail. *"Hello Miss, is it Miss Hilda? We have come from Redchop, from Mt Arackach and through Scattercorn by foot and we"*-- Leah was interrupted by a stern female voice *"It's Mrs, Hilda. So, tell me, have you seen him!?"* Hilda spoke like a displeased headmistress in a strict school. *"Seen who, Miss? Mrs, I mean."* asked Leah assuming the role of a troublesome student.

Nihal nudged her in the ribs, *"Amsel"* he said, through secretly pressed lips. *"I know,"* said Leah in return, *"I didn't know what else to say."* Hilda barked, *"I am talking of the man named Amsel, my husband of too many years now, have you seen him?"* *"Yes, we have been with him a few miles back that way. He gave us a drink and was very kind and helpful,"* responded Leah.

Hilda "*So he is still over there in his tent is he??*"

Leah "*Yes, he is still living there.*"

Hilda continued her interrogation, "*And what does he do all day?*"

Nihal and Leah were a little stumped by this questioning as they really didn't know the answer, they had never seen Amsel do anything in particular. There was of course evidence of his activities around the tent, his potions, his carvings, his notebooks, poems and singing, but they had never seen him actually do anything so to speak. Already feeling a little intimidated by the unexpected harshness of the lady, the two didn't want to upset her or risk a lie in support of Amsel. "*Well, well Mrs Hilda, he doesn't really do anything*"

"*Grraaa!! I knew it! I suppose he hasn't had a shave yet either? He still has that ridiculously large moustache?* she asked. "*He has a huge beard!* chirped Leah, who really liked Amsel's beard. "*Gah! A beard! He is hopeless! He will sit there forever without moving! Mulling over his endless and answerless questions. He is such a dreamer! He hasn't changed a bit,*" she said and threw her hand dismissively in the air in the direction of Amsel's corner of the forest, and turned away to go back inside. "*Come on you two, I have made some tea for you both, it's on the stove keeping warm, I had been expecting you.*"

Hilda led the way and they all walked inside, wiping their feet on the three doormats, each placed in front of the other like stepping stones. Each one read "Welcome" in a different language. Immediately inside the doorway was the kitchen, making it the entrance to the house. Dark wooden floorboards ran across the room perpendicular to the doorway, numerous patterned rugs were laying around in appropriate places, under the coffee table so as not to scratch the floor, by the sink so as to catch water and stop one's feet getting cold while washing, and so on. The ceiling had exposed rafters with white plaster in between, the walls were a mixture of wallpaper from the ceiling to head height and the lower half exposed brick. There was a wooden trim detailed with intricate carvings similar to what they had seen at Amsel's place. The house had a hospitable warmth of its own, greeting them with open arms. *"Come now, sit down,"* Hilda said, pulling out two chairs from the table in the centre of the room. They sat down and Hilda scurried off to complete the making of tea. Nihal and Leah looked at the table in front of them, all fantastically arranged, neat and tidy: the pens and pencils in separate colour-coded pots, the newspapers stacked neatly, a little note pad next to them with a daily list, and a glass half full of water sitting atop cork coasters. They looked at one another, noticing the stark contrast between Amsel's way of living compared with Hilda's. They were, on the face of it, the complete opposite.

"Now, here is your tea." Hilda moved very quickly using the smallest of steps, like a mouse she scurried to and fro without making a sound. She poured out the tea into three fine china cups and placed each on a saucer. Arranging them so all of the handles were facing the same way. She poured herself the last cup and sat down in the chair opposite, facing her table arrangements and notepad. *"Now if you wouldn't mind, please do tell me, what did Amsel say to you?"* Hilda's delivery was extremely calm and unique in the sense that it conveyed no emotion, yet as she spoke her fingers were rigidly gripping the tea cup, as though a certain strain existed. She was trying to keep her cool, Leah felt.

Nihal preferred to stay out of this and remained quiet, giving Leah a little kick under the table with his foot. *"He said rivers do not flow to the sea in a straight line,"* Leah said, avoiding any specific details. She continued on for a few minutes with an account of their stay, not mentioning Amsel's comments regarding Hilda. Hilda listened carefully, never interrupting, and appearing to be soaking up Amsel's words for herself in a seemingly soothing, or therapeutic way. It was as though he was speaking to her through Leah and his words, and voice, made her feel at ease.

"Oh he is so wonderfully hopeless" she said, slumping back into her chair. *"I do miss him so much. I wish he wasn't so damn lazy! He will just sit there dreaming and let things fall apart around him, just so he*

has something new to think about. 'It's meant to be this way or it wouldn't be so,' he would say, 'And yes it's meant to be so that I am here to fix it!' I would reply and he would laugh with his charming smile and I would forgive every time. The damned lazy git. Oh, I do miss him so much!" Hilda softened as she spoke of him, as if he was in her memories cuddling her. *"More tea? Would you both like some more tea?"* she asked, leaning forward again.

"Yes please, Miss Hilda! It was lovely, thank you!" Nihal offered his cup hastily, forgetting to refer to her as Mrs. Leah positioned her cup next to Nihal's, asking for a refill too. As they sat there drinking their tea, they could see that Hilda found the silence awkward. When she was not talking of Amsel she became fidgety and would begin to scan the newspapers in front of her looking for something to read and discuss. Nihal and Leah both sat silent, enjoying the tea and admiring Hilda's beautiful house and its interior. *"Did he give you an elixir?"* Hilda asked out of the blue. The two friends nodded to say yes. *"Oh he did?"* beamed Hilda. *"What was it?"* she asked. *"He gave us Mt. Arackach,"* Leah and Nihal said together in reply. *"Oh that was my favourite!"* said Hilda, with a smile.

A strong gust of wind blew through one of the shutters and knocked over some of Hilda's plants and pottery. Crashing to the floor, it broke into many pieces. *"Oh my, the wind is picking up rather nastily, isn't it?"* She looked very concerned as she closed the shutters again and fixed them shut with a leather strap. *"It's a little early for a wind like that, I hope everything is ok."* Hilda tidied the broken pieces of the pot and swept up the soil that was left on the floor. She sat back down to the table, pouring out the last of the tea. *"How was your tea, my darlings?"* she asked again and nodded suggestively as she filled the cups *"It was lovely, thank you ever so much,"* said Nihal. *"Yes, it was lovely. Thank you for your kindness, Mrs. Hilda,"* smiled Leah sweetly.

"Oh, not at all! It's nothing really. It is the least I could do. I think you both may need a nap now, perhaps? Come follow me." Hilda led them both to a tiny staircase stuffed between the kitchen and a small living area. The steps were wood, again carved in the style of Amsel, the railing was steel and the whole thing was laced with a thick leather trim so palms were comfy when placed on it. Hilda was at the top of the stairs before Leah had managed two steps. *"Come on you two, time is of the essence, the wind is returning, and some rest will do you some good!"* Hilda shouted down from upstairs. They hopped up the stairs, Leah first, and on the fourth level they came into a small attic room with a chimney stack running through the centre. This placed it directly above the kitchen. The walls were covered in photographs of a young couple. Some were black and white and others more recent, full of colour. In the room were two single beds, one on either side of the room, both neatly made up by Hilda with fresh cotton bedding and silk pillows. There was a small stool at the foot of each bed with a pair

of knitted woollen socks. In the corner was a small makeup cabinet, made of drail wood. Leah could see on the desk a selection of creams and cosmetics which looked to be homemade. *"Did you make these?"* asked Leah *"Oh, yes I did. I use herbs and other extracts which I collect from the forest,"* replied Hilda. Leah walked over and picked up one of the containers and smelled it. *"It smells lovely!"* she said. She noticed on the desk there was a stack of envelopes and letters, some not yet opened. They were covered in markings that looked like crow's feet. There were hundreds of them. Leah could see from the letters which had been opened that they were signed *"Yours always, Amsel."*

The wind rattled at the window and Leah turned round to face Hilda and Nihal again. Hilda walked over to close the shutter for what was the only window in the room. *"I hope everything is OK."* she said as she closed it. The room became darker with the loss of light and Hilda lit the oil lamp that was hanging from the ceiling which gave off a warm, orange glow. *"Is that you?"* asked Nihal, pointing to one of the photos on the wall. There was a portrait of a beautiful girl looking at them. She sat on some rocks by the sea with a woven basket filled with what looked like seashells. Hilda took the picture gently from the wall and brought it close to her chest affectionately, *"Yes, it's me,"* and she smiled with nostalgia. *"They're all me. This is me when I was one, this is me when I left school. This is me with my best friend as we came home one day covered in mud from the fields, this is me and this is my Amsel,"* she held a photo of a dashing young man, tall and chiselled like a statue. He was tucked into a sharp suit and had a large moustache between his nose and top lip. *"This is my Amsel,"* she said again and passed the picture over to Leah. *"And this is us when we married,"* she continued, passing her this picture too. The photo captured them both in dashing wedding attire. Hilda was wearing a large diamond ring, and beads and pearls followed her perfectly defined shoulders and neck. Immaculate and precise, every inch of the photo was perfect. They were the perfect couple. Just like every girl dreamed of. Nihal handed the photo over to Leah for her to have a look. *"You are beautiful, Mrs Hilda. I hope one day I am married, too, in such a beautiful way"* said Leah. Hilda smiled and thanked her and sat down on a stool.

She appeared to be very calm and relaxed. *"Why aren't you living together anymore?"* asked Leah. Thinking of her own parents and how they had separated, how her mother had kept nothing of her father around except his tool chest that she had herself a use for. Hilda let out a sigh, *"I just love him too much,"* and she hurriedly took all of the photos back and placed them back on the wall neatly. She walked over to the dressing cabinet and began to file her nails. She was silent and thoughtful for a moment, *"It's like a really good party. You come, you have a good time, and you leave feeling worse than when you arrived. That's love!"* she exclaimed. *"Things are never so simple when men are involved. It's not like loving your plants or your pets, they will predictably love you back. men are not so simple,"* she said, checking her nails *"In the end though, you learn: everything that you do to others, you do it to yourself. I love my Amsel, dearly."*

Hilda finished with her nails and made her way back to the stairs *"How did you know?"* asked Leah. *"How did you know we were going to be arriving?"* Hilda smiled and nodded towards the window where the wind rattled. A small mouse was sat on the ledge peering in. It sniffed the air and scurried off from sight. The birds were above the house, the ravens were swirling. The friends slept a restful sleep and set off bright and early the next day.

The King

He sat rigid as a statue, fingernails biting into the cap of his throne's wooden armrests, worn and gnawed at over years and now resembling crumbling bark. He had red hair and a thin beard with slightly sunken cheeks and a chiselled but balanced jaw and chin. His symmetrical features were of maturity, mystery and depth. On his head sat a rusting crown, fashioned after something much grander than the base metal from which it was made, now painted in a red soot of rust, the colour of which matched his hair. The rust smeared his brow red. He sat looking out onto a grey shimmering lake, and he appeared focused on something, although there was nothing apparent for him to look at. Leah and Nihal walked over to him and introduced themselves confidently. They were both rather bolder than they had been when they had first set out, for they had already seen so much. *"Hello Sir, I'm Leah and this is Nihal, my friend. We have come from Womblotian and Scattercorn and Mt Arackach. We are just passing through this way as we are now heading home."* Without turning his head or body in acknowledgement of them, The King replied with an unmoved and distant voice, *"There are no children in Scattercorn, or Arackach or Womblotian. Where are you from children?"* he asked. Nihal replied, *"We are from Redchop,"* punching the air symbolically.

The King's brow creased, leading to a squint and a raised left cheek, his head turned from the top with his eyes and his face followed. *"You are from Redchop?"* he asked. *"Yes,"* said the two at once. *"Redchop, the old place on the edge of the fields, which sits at the base of the mountain Arackach? It has been many years since I gathered myself there one late evening. I'd been passing through on my horse as king. The people there are of good nature, straightforward and genuine, too concerned with work and toil for wandering, or wondering for that matter. I remember that a fine lady gave me food, and the horse some hay and water. We stayed a short while. Was the clocktower still broken?"* asked The King. *"Broken, what do you mean broken?"* Nihal butted in before Leah could ask the same. *"When I passed through the clocktower was not working, and there was a certain commotion to the place as a result because nobody knew the time, or the date. The business schedules and the news radio were affected. This commotion and bustle was very charming at the time, and I believe it added somewhat to my memory of the place."* The King said in his clear tonality. *"When was this?"* asked Leah. *"Many many years back now, before you were alive, I am sure. It was only a few seasons since The Kingdom had fallen."* As he spoke his hands clutched at the chair armrests with frustration visible between his knuckles, his fingernails sank into the wood. His shoulders raised with tension, he felt pain as he spoke of his kingdom, *"The Kingdom had fallen, and I had moved on. On from my material throne and on to another, that of nobility,"* finished The King. *"What do you mean, Sir? You moved from kingship to nobility? The Kingdom fell and you became a noble? I don't understand,"* asked Leah, probing the apparent misconception. *"He said that without his kingdom and riches he found nobility."* Nihal whispered to Leah. *"Largely correct, boy,"* said The King. *"When my kingdom fell my servants left and my royal jewels were stolen and sold. Much had been lavished on me since birth. Then I was left only with that which I carried in my satchel upon my horse."* He looked to the left, a leather satchel hung from a branch of a nearby tree just a few yards away. *"Oh that's awful!"* said Leah.

"Well child it was, for a short time. At first, I was bitter and resentful, a treasonous betrayal, you see. Nothing felt pleasing to me! But, the more I was away from it the more I realised a king is merely the manifestation of his subjects. They define his being. Design and control him, in a sense. I learned that slaves rule slaves, and kings rule kings. I wanted to be King of Kings!" he pronounced strongly. *"How can a king rule kings? I thought kings were at the top?"* asked Nihal.

The King continued, *"That's right, boy. They are. But if your subjects are also kings then this makes you the King of Kings. Regardless, beyond The Kingdom I found much more than I had imagined. Out of my failed kingship came a new-found life, new strength, and feelings I'd not encountered before. I had been defined by my wealth and all those cynical blessings from strangers. You see, when a stranger loves you, you become a stranger. Their eyes, millions of them watching you, you become nothing but them. Today, when I meet a person they do not praise me, for they have no reason to. They barge past as though I didn't matter anymore than the soil under their boot or the plants they'd trodden down. It was at first unsettling, but this grew into a feeling of wholesomeness for me, that I as a man was indeed just like the soil under boot and the plants that grew beneath. I was amongst them. I was everywhere and alive, I felt. I was no longer a stranger and I began to feel closer to the people."* The King paused a little, looking at the lake with a distant eye that brought his memories to him.

"As I became used to this normalcy, the smells of nature became richer. I acquired a new sensitivity. I began as I do, to seek new stimulations from this. The richness I encountered in those early days of apparent peasantry had been so exhilarating that I craved more. I realised I had quickly fallen into my old self-seeking stimulation, this time not in the regal delicacies of kingship but the gritty harshness of peasantry. As it turned out, there was no difference between being The King of the peasants and being a peasant itself. My greed was rampant no matter what! So, I placed myself here into the wilderness, away from all that had enslaved me in my kingship, and all that had liberated and thrilled me in peasant life. The harshness of the weather here bites in all seasons. Wintery hail thrashes my face so I feel pain. Spring brings strong wind from the lake. In the summer it's hot and I sweat. The autumns are humid and damp, and the mosquitoes, I can't stand them!" He slapped an insect that landed on his neck. *"I feel*

alive here, a different feeling from behind a window pane and close to a fire, or flipping pages through a book on life and how to live, how to be educated. We had in the castles great libraries on how to behave and how to think. I lost many years as such, shielded from a world of nobility."

"You would rather sit here on your wooden throne on your own, all day long, than be a king? What about the food and the banquets?" asked Nihal, dumbfounded in spite of the king's explanations. *"A king of slaves, boy, I told you. The king of the slaves is the greatest of the slaves,"* responded The King. *"He is crazy, Leah,"* whispered Nihal to Leah.

The King stood up and walked over to a fire that crackled a few metres away. He knelt and poured some water from a flask into a shallow, concave saucepan that looked handmade and overused. There was a puff of steam as the water hit the metal. He shuffled the pan into the crackling embers of the fire so it was stable. He stood and walked over a few yards to the pine trees that grew close by and picked the most recent needles from the tips of the branches. He dabbed the broken edge on his tongue, tasting a number of shoots. He selected a branch and calmly cut it away with a dazzling and sparkling sword pulled from a scabbard that had been hidden amongst his old clothing. He then returned it immediately. Walking back over to the fire, he stripped the needles from the branch by pulling it through his closed fist, and the needles fell into the bubbling water which immediately turned a rusty red colour. *"It's the same colour as your crown, Sir,"* said Leah. *"That it is, child,"* said The King and he took his rusty crown from his head, allowing his long red hair to fall across his face.

He was a beautiful man, not a day past thirty-three it seemed, and the passion in his blue eyes glowed brightly. Abruptly, he threw the crown to one side and it fell to rest amongst the undergrowth. *"I never thought I'd wear a crown of iron,"* he chuckled, squatting by the fire and stirring the brew with a wooden spoon. *"What happened though, Sir, why did The Kingdom fall in the first place?"* asked Leah. The King stood up and walked over to his satchel. *"Only two,"* he said, as he pulled out two small tin cups. He gave them one each and squatted again next to the fire, hands together and fingers locked.

The King spoke up, *"The story is long and I prefer not to revisit it with children."* He spoke with a smile and glint in his eye, as though he fondly remembered this turbulent period in his life. He looked over at his throne sitting by the lake. *"I will tell you when you are older, my child, and it is important to remember, I am still The King!"* He cast his arm over towards the lake with satisfaction and he concluded, *"It was here that I became the man my father wished me to be. It was here that I became The King!"*

Leah spoke to Nihal quietly as The King turned his eyes back to the fire and poured out some of the liquid into the two cups. *"He reminds me of Amsel, Nihal. He talks about things in a similar way. I wonder if they are related somehow?"* she said. *"Who knows, Leah, I still think he is crazy!"* said Nihal. *"Here you are children,"* said the King, offering them their warm drinks. They accepted and took a sip of what was a sweet, maple-like flavoured water. As they sat there looking out into the lake, Leah couldn't help but think about what The King had said about Redchop, regarding the broken clock.

Nihal woke up to the sound of a fish or bird slapping in the water. It was very early, and the lake was flat and shone white like a mirror. A light pink in the sky from the sunrise and misty translucence gave the horizon a fluorescent glow, like a veil had been draped across it. The King was asleep in his chair, and Leah was curled in a ball next to him. *"Leah, we must have fallen asleep. Let's get going. It's a beautiful morning!"* whispered Nihal, and Leah woke calmly. *"I was dreaming about home, Nihal, they were fixing the clock back home,"* said Leah. She stood up and rummaged in her pocket. *"I'm going to give this to The King, it's one of Amsel's poems. The one that the raven gave to me,"* she said, and pulled the folded piece of paper from her pocket. Leah bent over to the sleeping king and tucked it into his robe. They set off.

"Children, before you go, you must make a wish," said the King, who had woken.

A little startled, thinking he had been still asleep, Leah responded *"OK!"* and she closed her eyes and made a wish. *"Thank you King!"* said Nihal, making a wish, too. They waved and set off again. The King looked out at the glowing lake and noticed the folded paper tucked into his robe.

He picked it out and unfolded it, he read:

"

You can be frugal,

And thrift,

Find a remote satisfaction in what you call yourself, allow yourself to drift,

Between two posts, conveniently placed either side of what you expect to achieve, nothing less-nothing more,

This way, as your guarantor,

You guarantee in your mind, a little corner of life for keeping yourself safe,

It is then much easier, to move with haste, in the direction that reinforces your little wooden posts that sit either side of you, forced into the broken soil and easy for you to talk about,

This way they say,

Is what you ought to be,

But though,

Where has it gotten you, and them?

Esoteric teachings, practised by everything that isn't human, all the ambitions of the alchemist part of the daily routine of the seasons of earth,

She does birth-a wide array of condiments for us to garnish and flavour our existence,

But as mentioned before, you currently prefer the posts, easier to then boast and compare and reference with another human,

Human,

What is it that we mean when we say this word, have we really considered its significance and what it is that differentiates us as humans from that which we like to refer to as animals?

Arts and culture, of course, not hard to answer and no nothing to do with cunning, something a snake with cold blood can manage twice a day,

I say,

We carry our history forward,

We do not die at death,

That last painfully slow gurgling breath-Is not your death-you may leave to those you love,

Cultivate a community,

Plant some seeds,

A pretty flower that's there again for another to see,

To smell,

To pick,

And to pass on to a beautiful lover,

Who'll one day be a mother,

To another- like you,

And this will suffice,

There are many options for joy in your life-to share,

Human,

Next spring, for instance,

If you've enough subsistence,

Take your garden path and take the garden hoe,

To the soil, to the seeds,

The seeds that you did sow,

Feel your arms work the soil and feel the nobility in this toil-It's work-it hurts,

It then cleanses your heart,

This is how-right from the start-we gave,

And so, we became,

A Human,

A Noble,

Who could fear and love the sun for both warmth and drought and feel both,

The rains for thirst and flood,

To drink fresh water in thirst,

To feel thirst,

To do real work,

It was available to us then,

So-human, yes there is the strife,

But your last gurgling breath is not your death,

And remember,

Fill your heart with this feeling,

Let it flow in its purpose,

Until you're fast again prescribed the pressing certainty that you are going to die anyway and that it doesn't matter,

And you just then stop,

Ask to replace that which is your so called life, your posts,

Replace this with service,

Service to that which was always here humming before you could weep a single tear out of selfish love or fear,

That which is here,

Before us and has trust,

From animals and from earth,

From us,

Now In yourself believing it,

Just as when every farmer casts his seed he does so in the knowledge that it will grow,

And be cropped to feed all friend and foe,

And so, again,

Your last breath is not your death,

Up there now the Man is walking the night,

Holding a pitcher of water, pouring into the sky to nourish mans breed,

All that have listened- and learned,

And take heed to these stars at night,

In its grandness and magnitude and not taken in selfish fright,

Those who allowed it all in,

You must copy this behaviour and allow all joy and gratitude to fill you,

Be fanatically obedient and devoted to your new service,

For it is what you are,

You are a slave of good,

Dear Human,

Your new and old joy of belonging,

You see."

The wishing well

Winter was drawing close, it could be seen clearly in the shades of autumn, as golden browns became deeper and blacker. The earth under foot that in the summer they had trodden as fine soil, soft like milled flour in the sun, was now frozen solid. The ground was cold enough and the sky dark enough that plant life decided it was time to leave. They would pack up their things and dump everything that they didn't need on the floor. The last leaves fell, leaving only the wire frames for them to return to and rebuild the following spring. The winter had arrived quickly. *"To be honest, Leah, it would be nice to be at home now. My haystack would be so warm and cosy, just sitting there with a pot of tea! I miss my dogs as well!"* said Nihal.

After such a journey, their appetite for adventure had waned a little. Being at home would be rather pleasant, they thought. *"I wonder how Mum is,"* said Leah. *"It would be nice to see her, I hope she is ok and not too worried! I never told her I was leaving. I miss her."* Nihal agreed and said, *"I didn't tell my dad either, I'm going to be in trouble."*

The two walked on and began paying less and less attention to their surroundings, and for the most part, they locked on to the path they were now treading. In their minds was home and the thought of being back dragged them forward. They walked much faster and felt rushed. There was a big frozen lake up ahead. *"There is a shortcut across the ice, Nihal,"* said Leah. *"How do you know Leah?"* asked Nihal. *"I just do. You can see that the woods curve around it anyway so, if we go across it'll save us some time,"* Leah responded.

Nihal, *"Are you sure?"*
Leah, *"Yes of course!"*
Nihal, *"Is it safe?"*
Leah, *"Yes, of course, it's frozen! Look!"*
Nihal, *"Ok you first then!"*

Leah stepped out onto the lake and walked forward a few metres. *"See, it's fine!"* she said assuredly. No sooner had she spoken and the ice began to crack like lightning across the lake surface. *"Quick, Leah, run!"* shouted Nihal, fearful that Leah would soon fall in. As she ran, the ice broke and one of Leah's feet fell through, she tripped forward in a panic. The ice continued to crack and shatter around her in a circle, as she lay flat on her face crying.

"Leah. Come on! Get off the ice!" shouted Nihal again. Leah picked herself up and was able to make it the last few metres back to the

riverbank. A large sheet of ice broke off and freezing water flowed to the surface of the lake where Leah had fallen in.

Nihal, *"That was close, Leah, I thought you were going to fall in and die!"*
Leah, *"Me too!! That was scary!"*
Nihal, *"I said it didn't look safe."*
Leah, *"Shut up! No need to rub It in! My foot is wet!"* she said, shaking her foot.
Nihal, *"I know but I did say so."*
Leah, *"Come on, let's go anyway, I need to move around and warm up."*

They walked for a while and came to a clearing, what would have been a blooming meadow in the spring. In the clearing there was a well with a path leading to it through the grass. *"Look, Leah, a wishing well!"* shouted Nihal with excitement. *"Let's get a drink and make a wish!"* Leah said *"Yes, let's!"*

They ran through the meadow and over to the well that burrowed itself deeply into the ground. It was an old well, there was no roof or bucket, just a hole with some large stones built up around its brim, and a rusted iron bar fixed across. Presumably for a rope and bucket that no longer existed. They stopped and sat on the ledge, dangling their legs over the edge. Nihal tossed in a stone, *"One, two, three, four,"* he counted the seconds before it splashed into the water at the bottom. *"Four seconds was four miles of lightning, that was what Womblot said!"* exclaimed Nihal. *"Yes, but it's not lightning, Nihal, it's a stone in a well. It's not that deep! The King said to make a wish. You first!"* said Leah. Nihal peered in, leaning forward, and the large stone he was sitting on gave way beneath him. *"Nihaal*!!!" Screamed Leah as Nihal slid into the well. *"Nihalll!"* Leah screamed again. *"Leah,"* choked and spluttered Nihal, *"I can't swim Leah!!"* Leah threw herself onto her stomach with her arms over the side of the well. She lay there reaching in as far as she could, tearing her arms from her shoulders but it was too deep for her to be able to help. *"Nihal!!"* she screamed. Her screams echoed down and back up with the sounds of splashing, and then silence. Deafening silence.

Leah's head dropped forward and she banged her nose on the well's stone wall, bloodying it. She was consumed by shock. She rolled off the edge of the well and fell onto the grass in a heap. She began to crawl away from the well on her stomach, heaving herself along like a wounded soldier on a battlefield. She was whaling and was engulfed by pain. Her blood had withdrawn from her skin and limbs, her heart demanded so much for survival. Her fingers bent inwards and cramped, digging into the soil that was between her and hell. She screamed with pain and flipped onto her back, screaming into the sky, *"No!!"* She grabbed her face with her muddied hands, her fingernails digging into her cheeks. Laying on the ground, she looked like a discarded doll that had been thrown from a passing car window into the mud. The trees bent inwards and over towards her, such was the gravity of her pain. She got up and ran. She ran back the way they had come, back towards the lake. As she got to its bank she could see that the ice had melted and the lake lay still. She fell to her knees crying, her blood simmering like acid in her veins. The pain corroded her joints and she felt as though she would unravel like a spiral of ribbons into the sky. She screamed once more, *"Nihal! Why!"* As she knelt there screaming, she heard a voice in her mind, *"Come to us"*. The lake turned black like tar. She felt it calling her in. *"Come to us,"* it said loudly in her mind, *"Come to us,"* ushering her in to end her pain, it felt so gentle, welcoming and safe. She raised herself to one knee to make her way into the black lake. A flock of ravens flew above her and out towards the dead trees that protruded from the centre of the lake. They swooped down and vanished, and at that moment a weight was lifted from Leah's chest. She could breathe again. The lake immediately turned white and froze over. Her eyeballs rolled back in her head and she passed out.

Leah regained consciousness to find herself walking. Neck folded forwards and in a buckled posture. One foot in front of the other, like a zombie. Leah walked in the night. She was cold, lonely and numb. She stopped to raise her head. She was muddy and underneath white like a ghost. Her face was white and blue from the freezing cold tears that drenched it, and dry blood smothered her nose and mouth. Ahead not too far in the distance, she could see a silhouetted figure standing amongst the black bushes. Staring straight at her. *"Come closer,"* a voice entered Leah's mind. *"Come closer, come to us,"* again it rang behind her eyes, vibrating a chill along her spine, *"Come to us."* Leah placed one foot in front of the other, drawn forward, just a dirty sheet blowing in the wind. As she got closer the voice became louder. *"Come closer, come close,"* it beckoned her. *"I'm coming,"* whimpered Leah, with a tearful, timid voice. Cold droplets of water fell on her from the branches above as she pushed slightly into the bushes where the figure was standing. She wiped her face.

The figure had gone. *"Was it ever there?"* she wondered for a moment. Directly in front of her was a tree. A huge tree. Its bark creased like the face of an old man after a lifetime of expression, and it looked straight at her, but the voices had stopped. There was nothing to be heard other than the bats flickering in the moonlight above her. Leah wailed in pain. *"Why!"* she whimpered in suffering, sniffling with tears. *"Why did this happen to you Nihal? I'm so sorry,"* and she collapsed forward onto the tree, embracing it like her father... she had not thought of him in years. She wrapped her arms around it and held as tight as she could, so it could never leave her. *"What did I do wrong? What do I need to do? What is next for me?"* she stammered and whimpered, pressing against the rough bark which ground into her face. There wasn't a sound to be heard in reply. *"Why don't you answer me?"* Leah wailed, hugging the tree and she cried into the night until she lost consciousness.

Going home

Leah came to and found herself walking again, dragging her feet as though they were weighted with lead and there was no real point in moving them, for she was already drowned. One in front of the other. On and on she went. *"I might as well stop and die,"* she thought to herself as she made her way home. She felt crushed, collapsed inwards like the brightest star, now just a black hole consuming everything that had been created before it. She moved with a hunched back, aged a million years. Her fur coat was discoloured, worn and haggard, and her hair was now a knotted brown mess like an old rug. She had made a mistake, she thought, and this was the worst feeling. An aching, regretful feeling, a resentment for herself. She blamed herself for Nihal's death and she felt as though she had failed him. She regretted leaving in the winter before. *"Those stupid birds,"* she thought to herself, *"that stupid clock! I can't believe I did this!"*

She hobbled onwards down the road to Redchop, the western road, opposite to the side of the village they had left from. Rain fell drumming dramatically on the cobbles, a grand entrance for her. She was wet through, but she didn't care about how she felt anymore. The uneven cobbled path made it difficult to walk with her aching and exhausted legs. She ambled on as best she could. Looking around, Redchop was just the same as she had left it and smoke seeped out of the chimneys into the early morning air. With the sky still dull it looked like snow ascending upwards. As she got closer to the town centre she saw a group of adults smoking outside the newspaper printers. They were always at work extremely early as they had the most important job in Redchop. She looked downwards to hide her face, not wishing for any attention. One of the men shouted over *"Hey, are you OK?"* he said. Leah froze suddenly. She hadn't spoken to anyone in days and didn't want to. The adults would usually ignore her and she couldn't remember anyone paying any attention to her when she left, even as she marched past them in the snow with no shoes on, all those months ago. *"Hey are you OK, there?"* the man asked again and started to walk towards her. Leah looked apprehensive and gave a few nods of her head in succession and held out her palms and said, *"I'm OK, please, I'm OK. I just want to go home"*. The man understood and stopped his advance. *"Well, just get yourself home then, child, it's cold out, you look terrible,"* he said. Leah continued to walk down the street. She couldn't understand why this man had cared about her, what was the difference between now and when she had left? She had shoes, a coat, and there was no snow on the ground. Why was she given attention now and not before?

As she walked through Redchop she could see there were birds nesting on the rooftops, and they chirped as she walked by. She walked on, past the last terrace of houses and into the square by the church. She looked up at the clock. It was 11:13 in the morning. She carried on and finally arrived at her mother's house. She was home at last. Leah muddled her way around the house and went to the side door, so as not to be noticed. She stood in the doorway and listened to the rain patter on the porch tiles, tapping the ground as they ended their journey from sky to earth. Leah pushed the door ajar and stepped in. A warm gust of air hit her face as she entered the hallway. The kitchen stove was burning and she could smell her mother's morning coffee. She hobbled into the house which felt so welcoming and safe. As she moved through the hallway she saw her mother's picture hanging, that same picture she had studied all the winter before. *"Leah my dear. Leah, where have you been!?"* her mother shouted and ran out of the living room with her arms open, overwhelmed with happiness to see her daughter home safely. *"Where have you been, my Leah! Where have you been? I was so worried about you!"* Leah's mother pushed her frail fingers into her shirt pocket and pulled out a cotton handkerchief with a pretty leaf pattern. She wiped Leah's cuts, bloodied nose and muddied cheeks to reveal a little of the girl she knew underneath. *"Where have you been, Leah, where have you been, what happened to you?"* All Leah wanted to do was say sorry and cry in her mother's arms. *"I'm sorry Mum. I'm sorry,"* the words got stuck in her throat.

Leah couldn't talk, she was feeling too overwhelmed. She looked at her feet and walked into the kitchen, her head hanging in shame. Her mother stepped in front and pulled out a chair for her and then quickly put the kettle on. *"Leah you must be thirsty, and hungry. We need to get you out of these clothes! I'll make you a hot drink and we can talk. I have been so worried about you."* Leah's mother was frail and old and this was the most alert Leah had seen her in a very long time, her love and joy for her daughter was glowing fervently . She had not felt this kind of love from her mother since she was young. Leah sat herself down slowly onto the kitchen chair that her mother had pulled out for her. It was too tall for her, and her feet hovered slightly above the floor. She looked at her palms which were muddy and with cracked skin. She turned her hand over to inspect the other side. Her fingernails were black with dirt and there was peeling skin and cuts all over them. She felt awful and her head spun like a kaleidoscope.

"What can I do now?" she thought to herself. Her mother was going to want an explanation, and how was she ever going to tell Nihal's father? Could she really tell the truth? Could she tell her mother that Nihal was dead and that she wished she was, too? She couldn't tell her mother. She didn't have the strength. Leah gulped, clenching her face in discomfort as she tried to remain somewhat composed. *"Here is some warm milk sweetheart, it's not too hot, drink it now. It's just warm enough, the way you like it,"* Leah's mother placed a jug and two cups in front of her. She wiped the sides and sat down next to her

daughter. *"So, tell me what happened,"* Leah's mother smiled endearingly at her daughter who looked distraught and lost in the home she had grown up in. Leah still couldn't speak. *"Do you remember what happened darling, can you remember? Has someone hurt you?"* Her mother asked. *"No,"* muttered Leah. Her mother stood up and went over to the cabinet in the corner of the kitchen. Leah sat there somberly with her hair draped over face. There was a newspaper on the table. Leah's mother pushed the paper in front of Leah. Leah moved an eye in acknowledgement. She took a minute, and looked more carefully.

The front page had a picture of the church. *"Church bells stop and clock face breaks"* the headline read, featuring a picture of a scaffold around the clock tower and with men working on it. *"The day you left, the clock stopped working. They think the wind had blown so strongly that the glass broke on its face. It had happened only once before, many years ago. I had been in Redchop only a few days at the time. That's the day I met your father, he had arrived on a horse."* said Leah's mother.

At that moment the church bells started to ring loudly and there was a knock at the door. *"Let me get that,"* said Leah's mother, and she walked over to the door. She opened it and there stood Nihal, absolutely soaking wet. *"Nihal, what are you doing here!? Leah just arrived a minute ago."* Leah's mother turned towards the kitchen and before she had a moment to speak, Leah had ran through the kitchen and pounced onto Nihal with open arms, clinging to him with hugs and kisses. *"Nihal! Nihal!! I thought you were dead!"* laughed Leah, joyously in tears.

"Dead?" Leah's mum said, confused.

"I thought you were dead, Nihal, I can't believe you are here!!" laughed Leah, overwhelmed with jubilation.

Nihal was glowing with joy too, and said, *"A river ran under the well Leah, and I was washed up on the farm. I can't go home yet, my dad will be furious! Can I stay here and dry out a little?"*

The End

Printed in Great Britain
by Amazon

55637105R00069